+

Maria Dracula™

Maria Dracula ™

Volume I

Maria Dracula and the Vampire Kids

By

Alice Rose

DUENDE Books
Los Angeles, California, 2005-2007

Printed in the United States of America

Praise for Maria Dracula

* A previous version of Maria Dracula was a finalist in ForeWord Magazine's 2005 Book of the Year Annual Awards in Juvenile Fiction.

* "[Alice Rose] has a fun new series out for children." Read Jenie Franz' book review of Maria Dracula at MyShelf.com.

*Maria Dracula features as compulsory reading in the Syllabus for the English class at Milwood Elementary School in Kalamazoo, Michigan.

*In 2007 Maria Dracula is published in Romania by one of the most prestigious publishers of children's literature and textbooks, Editura Didactica si Pedagogica from Bucharest.

* Maria Dracula was on display at the Bologna Children's Book Fair 43rd edition, Bologna, Italy, March 27-30, 2006.

*Maria Dracula featured in the ForeWord Magazine March/April 2006 edition, at children's titles.

*Maria Dracula was on display at BookExpo America, Washington, D.C., May 19-21 2006

*Maria Dracula was on display at the Frankfurt Book Fair, Germany, October 4-8, 2006

*Maria Dracula featured in Bookmarks Magazine , 2006

*Maria Dracula on Internet:
- Official site: www.mariadracula.com
- Blog: www.mariadracula.blogspot.com
- Angela Ursillo's site: www.angelaursillo.com
- MyShelf.com
- Young Adult (& Kid's) Books Central
- Vampress.net
- DUENDE Books' website: www.duendebooks.blogspot.com

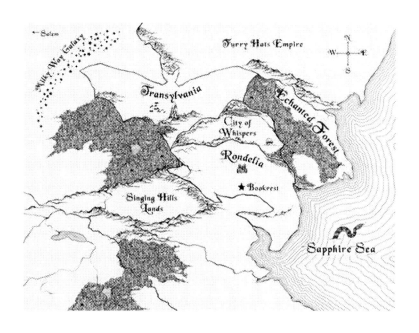

The MaP of Maria Dracula

Table of Contents

Acknowledgements

My gratitude goes to the many authors of children's books from various cultures — such as Hans Christian Andersen, Charles Perrault, Brothers Grimm, Carlo Collodi, Edmondo de Amicis, Jules Verne, Hector Malot, Mark Twain, L. Frank Baum, Robert Louis Stevenson, Petre Ispirescu, and Shahrazad — whose stories have delighted me as a child, opening a fantasy universe that many times has invited me to daydreaming I was boarding the first ship to a lost pirates' island in some Emerald Sea.

To Vlad, my parents, and my one-time elementary school colleagues also go my thanks, since they were my first story audiences.

I am grateful to Renni Browne, former senior editor for William Morrow, for her dedicated editing of many earlier versions of this book, Herta Feely and others who edited a earlier drafts of this book, and the writers- and poets-instructors in the Writer's Program at the University of California, Los Angeles.

Special thanks go to talented Angela Ursillo, whose illustrations have brought visual life to my book, making me see my characters with eyes other than the mind's.

This is a fantasy book written the way stories are told in Southeastern Europe, where surrealism supplants the gothic and Orient meets Occident in literature and art. It is a fantastic story parents and grandparents would tell their offspring, hoping that children will learn about poetical language, and that through adventurous voyages any kid can become a hero.

1. Marigold, the Last Herbs Witch of Salem

It all started yesterday. Mother began to vanish, disintegrating into little green articles I couldn't find later in her bed or in her bedroom. Her hair, her hands, her mouth disappeared. Last to go were her eyes. Her bed was left empty under her moss-green quilt. The pillow kept her head's shape – and, just for a second, her warmth.

When Dr. Lily Lavender, Salem's physician, entered Mother's bedroom and saw her vanished entirely, she declared her dead.

"Funny, that's not how herbs witches die, Marigold," she said. "Herbs witches return to green sap." She added that upon our deaths, our guild must reunite with all the herbs witches of the past who live in the grass, shrubs, and trees of the Ghostly-Trees Forest.

"It may be Friday the thirteen," Mayor Icelandia de Winter said, storming in, "but herbs witches simply do not become wind." She blew a cold breeze into the room, turning my face purple and my tears to ice.

I tried to say something, but words jammed in my throat. Besides, a black muddy footprint the shape of a bug near Mother's bed got my attention. How did it get there, for we never had such big black bugs in our house?

As I dropped lilies of the valley on her empty witch coffin, all I knew was that Mother was dead. I had become an orphan – the only orphan to live alone in an old cottage with an attic full of pointed hats, herb recipes, and catalogues with paintings of witches. The only orphan to become the last herbs witch of Salem.

The autumn nights are still hot like orange drops of lava, the Twisted-Wand District quiet like vanishing mist.

Herb recipes waft lavender and coriander through the dim attic and down the snail-shaped staircase, spreading memories and magic throughout my home. Uncut silence flows down from the sky, brushing my ears, slipping through my fingers like a silk sash. It covers the satin of the black knee-long dress Mother made for me last year.

Two green teardrops head toward my dimpled chin, washing my freckles, gathering around my mouth. I taste them: they're watery-sweet, as usual. As were Mother's tears when she told me that if she died she'd rise to the sky, from whence she'd watch over me disguised as a star.

Alone in my night-filled attic, I drag a scarlet wooden box with dragon carvings over to the window and climb on it, eager to glimpse the faraway stars. I lean and stretch to follow a falling star but lose my balance. The box jerks, slips from under my feet, and the next thing I know I'm sprawled on the floor covered in spider webs.

The box, now on its side, is locked, so I must find a way to open it. I snoop around in old hatboxes filled with ribbons, feathers, and pads, with scraps, batting, and cotton balls. I poke through empty wardrobes smelling of wax and lemon and dead moths. No keys – only another muddy footprint, like a big bug's, under the window.

I set about trying to jimmy the box's lock. I don't give up. What dangerous secrets could lurk inside? Maybe some maps leading to a forgotten land of dragons. I tap and scrape and turn the box around – until I push a button by mistake. The box twitches and the lid flings open with a squeak. There, on the dusty bottom, lies something rolled up.

A papyrus! I unfold it ever so gently, but it loses a corner, which scatters into fine yellow dust. I hold my breath: I'm looking at a letter scribbled with black calligraphy.

It has a red seal with the head of a dragon -- long fangs and scary eyes with vertical cat-like pupils. And its nose is fuming, probably from spitting fire.

I begin reading:

September 1, 19 - (the papyrus is torn here)

Honorable Dorothy, Grand Herbs Witch of Salem,

Circumstances beyond my control force me to contact you in such haste and without proper introduction.

The day when your family from Transcarpathia needs you has come. Your blood heritage calls upon you. There is little time left.

When the Autumn Equinox turns flowers to dust, and the last summer of the twentieth century surrenders to the Lady of Autumnal Leaves, what is left of your last ancestor will perish.

I will explain everything upon your arrival here.

Walls have eyes, winds have ears, evil is close.

I look forward to meeting you soon.

Yours cordially,
Dr. L. Acua, Esquire
Theater of Vaudeville, Bookrest, Rondelia

I read the letter again, but it doesn't make sense. Who is this Dr. L. Acua? Where is Rondelia? I've never heard of a relative outside of Salem, much less in Transcarpathia. Isn't Transcarpathia the land of vampires? Who's going to die on the autumn equinox? And what's all this got to do with Mother? And –

Someone -- or something -- jumps on my back. It clasps fluid, acrid-smelling hands around my neck.

Help! But who can help me, now that Mother is dead?

I struggle in vain to break free from the creature's fierce clutch. I can't breathe. The black arms slide slowly toward my left hand, toward the papyrus.

Oh, no. You won't get it! I may be just a little girl, but this letter is the last thing I have about Mother. I wave the papyrus in the air, hoping it will escape my assailant's thrust. The putrid stench and the other muddy hand keep choking me. How much longer can I resist?

The black fingers reach the papyrus. They seize it, and a victorious holler follows. But then the fingers touch the red dragon seal -- burn and melt. The creature hisses like a giant bug fallen into a bonfire.

Free , I take a huge breath and stare at the dark, bug-like creature melting into a sizzling puddle of mud. The foul stink is everywhere. Drops of mud splatter onto the attic's walls, trickle, melt, and die.

I'm still holding the papyrus in my left hand and a question mark big as the moon in my head. What's going on here?

My mysterious encounter from yesterday suddenly pops up in my mind. Just when I was about to open the gate to our ivy-wrapped cottage. A witch dressed in a black cloak, oozing an underworldly smell and wearing a deep hood that masked her face walked out of our house, bumped into me, and vanished around the next corner. Of course, I barely noticed her. With Mother being a Grand Herbs Witch of Salem, I've seen many a witch coming to ask for her potions with jasmine, coriander, and nasturtium. But the smell is the same. And the bug-like footprint from the attic is identical to the one I saw near Mother's bed.

"Strange, isn't it, Marigold?" Mother would say. "But we're witches. We don't believe in coincidences. We're great masters of spells."

Heartbroken and dizzy, I leave the attic and the papyrus locked back in the box. I don't want to risk carrying it around in its dried, brittle condition. I head for my room.

I stoop in front of the cracked oval mirror, shivering. I've always been afraid of that mirror because it shows me twisted and blown in a dozen fragments. And every time I glance in it, I quake, knowing I may awaken the ghost that lives in there. For who else would play pranks with my reflection?

I have no such problem with the square mirror in the bathroom, where I brush my teeth. No evil spirits live in whole, flawless mirrors.

Late at night, I finally tuck myself into bed. For the first time in my life I'm all alone in the house -- except for the kitchen lightbulbs that quarrel every evening before we switch them off, Mother's China teapot that blossoms every day with red, white, and yellow roses, my T-shirt with the live black cat Meow printed on it, and of course the ghost in the second-floor cracked oval mirror.

I imagine that Mother is here with me, that she smoothes my forehead and closes my eyelids. Before I reach the land of dreams, I take a last squint at my bedroom window. The falling star shines brighter than ever. I imagine the star is Mother, wishing me goodnight.

"Goodnight, Mother," I say.

I dream that a dreadful war shatters Salem, that vampires from Transcarpathia have taken over our town. What's worse, I am the one responsible for this disaster, because I've brought the vampires to Salem through the papyrus letter – which turns out to be some sort of magic gate.

Morning again. I'm glad the war from my nightmare hasn't left any dead bodies or traces of pillage in my room.

"Marigold, why don't you go find your relative from Transcarpathia?" a voice resembling Mother's tells me in my head.

Considering that today is already September 14, 1999, will I make it in time – in

. . . let's see, eight days? At least I won't miss school, for September is the month of the Harvest Holiday. But where is Rondelia?

In a hurry I dress in my flower-embroidered baggy jeans and favorite Meow T-shirt, which gently purrs on my body. I tuck my hair into a ponytail and grab my backpack, in which I've stuffed a few clothes, Mother's magic shell, my kaleidoscope, and my "I ? Salem" T-shirt with a black pointed witch hat on it.

Humming "The Little Witch Apprentice Song," I swoosh down the staircase for the entry door and hop on my pink bike. The cobblestones make my bike jolt and my voice tremble but I don't stop humming.

Salem, the town where I live, is smaller than the cities of skyscrapers stretching to the south but bigger than the hamlets of dwarves Mother said she once saw in northern Europe. So Salem is just the right size for a town of nice witches.

I was born here ten years ago and Mother was born here as well – like all good witches. Not like the wicked witches who roam around the Black Hollow Lake ten miles north of Salem, hiding in caverns and catacombs filled with the souls they've snatched. I've never been to the Black Hollow Lake, and I promised Mother I'd never go there. That is, until I reach thirteen – witch age – and pass the Witchcraft Test, thus rightfully becoming a good witch of the realm.

On my right I reach my school, the Pointed-Hats Wizardry School. In June I've completed fourth grade. I like my school, honest. I'm best in The Science of Herbs, Roots, and Weeds – which is no surprise, since I'm a herbs-witch apprentice.

In the morning we take lessons in Poisons, Great Medieval European Sorcerers, Witchcraft Poetry, and The History of the Salem Witches. But when the afternoon sunset brushes the sky with glowing orange, we learn to fly on brooms, talk to cats, find herbs, and fight using magic wands.

Once in a while, Mr. Londinium Oxford, a teacher from England, comes to our school. Bald and old, he likes to scare us with stories about dragons with three heads that spit fire and wield their heavy tails like hammers.

Bang! Bang! Bang! I imagine the dragons smashing to the ground an entire congregation of wicked witches.

"These dragons live in northern Europe's thick fir tree forests," Mr. Londinium Oxford says, stiff as a stick, "and fight the elves."

"Elves?" we say in chorus.

"Others dive in the ocean and live with the sharks, hunting sailors and mermaids."

"Mermaids?" we say.

"Like Marigold?" Chrysanthemum Crown, the lawyer's daughter and my old foe although she's a witch apprentice herself, points at me and giggles. "Nerd witch!"

The class laughs.

I can't see my face but I just know it's turning red. One day I'll show these buffoons who's the grand herbs witch of Salem!

As for Mr. Londinium Oxford, he never shows us any proof of these creatures' existence, except for some strange maps and a few scary dragon paintings he admits he made out of his imagination.

Around a corner, I nearly run into Mrs. Baguette Higgins from the Silver Dust Bakery. In the morning she delivers bread to our neighborhood, and her magic basket is always full with ladybug-shaped mint-chip buns, muffins baked with magical rain-tree grains, cookies spread with coconut and stardust.

"Marigold, I'm sorry about your mother." She hands me a two-hole egg-and-sesame bagel. "Please stop by my shop whenever you're hungry, will you?"

I tell her thank you, grab the bagel, take a big bite, and choke a bit on its sesame seeds. By the time I finish it, I've reached the three-story witch-hat-shaped ancient Museum of Sorcery.

This summer I've visited it twice. That's because they always bring in new exhibits showing the history and deeds of the Salem witches. The most fascinating piece I've seen is a two-century-old broom discovered in the Ghostly-Trees Forest, five miles from Salem. It's said the broom belonged to a warrior witch who fought in the great wars of the Ash River, in the Land of Endless-Night.

Now, the Land of Endless-Night is another story, but the broom had so many cuts on its handle that it made a strong impression on me.

I imagined the warrior witch fighting fiercely, flying at high speed on her broom, crossing the sky, looping, veering right and left, falling yet rising again, smashing the wicked witches with her wand but ultimately being wounded and dying at the gates of Salem, after saving us all.

The funny thing is, I always imagined myself as this great warrior witch: I was the one fighting, I was the one dying. I'd even cry, sorry I had been killed. But at the end of the day, I had become a hero.

From a block away I can smell Mrs. Snippety Smith's brown muffin-shaped Magic Cookies Chocolaterie.

The white, milk, and dark chocolates fall domino-style into configurations of castles, railroads, and bridges. And again the little sweet things fly, swooping and stretching across the window and back to the rear shelves, then toppling and rising anew, forgetting they're just chocolates and one day some kid like me will eat them all.

Enticed by their funny game, I leave my bike in the street, enter the shop smelling of cocoa, and ask for a milk chocolate. Dark and wrinkled, Mrs. Snippety Smith squints at me. How come, of all the people in the world, does she get to be the boss of chocolates?

Mrs. Snippety Smith thrusts her hand out for a doomed milk chocolate that happens to fly in front of our eyes, trying to land as a bridge over a river of dark chocolates. But Mrs. Snippety Smith is quicker. She snatches it, wraps it up in a purple sheet of paper, and tosses it over to me.

"Ahem. Heard about your mother," she says, her voice like a trombone's. "Don't stuff yourself with chocolate, you'll grow as fat as your mother's late cat."

Everybody knows I was given a colony of purple butterflies as a present for my tenth birthday. Unfortunately Mother's long-haired cat, Boulder, ate them all. That's how it got

8

fat. Mother said the butterflies kept flying in its stomach. That's why it died. Poor, greedy Boulder.

I flounce out of the chocolaterie, muttering about how much I hate that witch. And I don't even know what guild she's from. But as I mount my bike, something jerks inside my pockets. There's a white chocolate hidden in the left one, behind my handkerchief, and a dark chocolate nesting in my right, among keys and Salem square pennies. There's justice in this world!

I've just started on my bike when Mrs. Snippety Smith yells behind me, "What's this rush, Marigold? Don't you want your chocolate?"

I turn and grab it. I can't look into her eyes. What if she really is a wicked witch?

Mrs. Snippety Smith scowls at me. "Where do you think you're going, other than to the Witches Orphanage?"

I want to call back to her that it's none of her wicked business where I'm going. Instead, I yell "Watch out!" at Mrs. Lemonade Jones's yellow-haired daughters, who happen to play hopscotch on the cobblestones right in front of my bike.

Around the next corner, Mrs. Butterfly Brown, the gardener of the Talking-Benches Park, and Mrs. Rainbow Brent use magic wands to rearrange the roses, lilac, and amaryllis in front of the Salem Public Library of Witchcraft.

I hold my breath to avoid the numbing scents and walk in the library, which looks like a five-story-tall book.

Ms. Poetry Pickens sits at the front desk. She stamps library cards and leafs through books, checking on their covers and edges, listening to the rustling of their pages. A librarian today, Ms. Poetry Pickens used to be a poet so famous that for years her book *The Living Poetry of Salem* was compulsory reading at my school. Now she's almost blind, and the moths have eaten her gray, once white Professors' Guild coat.

"Pardon me, ma'am," I say, "I'm looking for information about Transcarpathia and Rondelia. Can you help me, please?"

"Of course, Marigold," she says, mounting her pince-nez with their distorted dioptric lenses on her nose. "My condolences for your late mother. She was a good witch. What a pity…" She coughs and peeks at a chart, then pushes a button. A

9

bookshelf from the back of the library bolts toward us with a squeak. It stops one foot from the front desk and pushes forward a book from its third shelf down. Ms. Poetry Pickens picks it up, checks its title, and hands it over to me. "There you are. A Fantastic Eastern Europe atlas."

I take refuge with the book in a lonely corner. I can't find a chair. I drop my backpack on the floor and sit on top of it, hoping I won't squeeze Mother's magic shell.

Unknown countries, mountains, and rivers flow from one page onto the next, as if the atlas were alive. Finally I find a map labeled Rondelia.

The country looks round and tailed, like a sunfish. It neighbors the bat-shaped Transcarpathia to the west, the Enchanted Forest and the Furry-Hats Empire to the north, the Singing-Hills lands to the south, the Sapphire Sea to the east, and the City of Whispers back in time.

As for Bookrest, Rondelia's capital, all I get from the atlas is a legend – about books. According to this myth, Bookrest once had the largest library in this part of the world. Rare volumes from Florence, Paris, London, and Berlin, from Prague, Delhi, Jakarta, and Tokyo sat silently on shelves that rose up to the sky. The fable says the gods read from this collection and learned about the hearts and minds of the humans. The tomes were alive, so the story goes, yet they rested in this city. Hence the name Bookrest.

Happy to learn that Rondelia promises to be an enchanted place – not the scary country with dragons I pictured upon reading the papyrus letter – I head out of the library.

Ms. Poetry Pickens doesn't acknowledge my farewell, caught up in stamping more books and propping her falling pince-nez on her thin shiny nose.

I hurry to the City Hall. Mayor Icelandia de Winter works there. The ten-story golden building resembles a magic wand with a five-pointed star on its top and a Salem witch-hat flag that flutters day and night.

Upon reaching the City Hall, I press my foot on the first step of the flight of stairs. "To the mayor's office, please," I say.

The staircase whisks me up to the third floor. It leaves me dizzy at the entrance of a brightly lit corridor and disappears back into the ground.

For a while I get lost in the hallway – none of the doors have names on them, except one at the far end.

I knock once and the door flies open. Mayor Icelandia de Winter stares at me. As usual, she's dressed in a long gown made of twirled flocks of wool, white-and-gray like the color of her spread hair. They say she was born in Iceland. That she commands the snowflake dance, the falling icicles, and the blizzard. That she protects Salem from heavy winters and has long ago befriended spring. Rumors say she's winter itself, but I think she's just a witch – a powerful one.

The room is stuffed with porous clouds of snowflakes, one right around Mayor Icelandia de Winter's head.

"What are you doing here, Marigold?"

"I want to go to Rondelia."

"But you're supposed to go to the Witches Orphanage, am I right?"

I sigh and nod.

"In, let's see. . .seven days, am I right?"

"No! In eight – the autumn equinox is in eight days."

Mayor Icelandia de Winter looks on a calendar with moving zodiacs, between Virgo and Libra. "You're right. September twenty-first is next Saturday. You're a smart little witch. I'm sure you'll do fine."

"But I want to go find my relative – "

"What relative?" Mayor Icelandia de Winter asks, her face turning blue from a cloud of ice that happens to melt on her hair.

I tell her all about the papyrus, my dream to reunite with my last living relative from Transcarpathia, and my need to get there quick. I'm not mentioning the bug-like creature that melted in my attic, afraid she might not let me go.

Mayor Icelandia de Winter ponders for a moment, then says, "But do you have a passport, little girl?"

"Sure I do."

"Let's see it. And your mother's signature on it."

"Signature?" I look at her again. With her bushy white eyebrows drawn together and her icy-translucent eyes peering at me through lowered eyelids, with her frostbitten-purple nose and her lips pursed over clenched teeth, Mayor Icelandia de Winter's face has practically turned into a blizzard.

"Your mother's signature, Marigold. You cannot leave Salem without it. You're a minor. And an orphan."

I leaf desperately through my passport, back and forth. Nothing. No signature.

Eyes swollen with tears, I'm back on the magic stairs.

I'm going down, and then back home to pack for the Witches Orphanage. Mrs. Snippety Smith will surely poke fun at my failure. I wanted so much to go to Bookrest, and now I've missed my only chance to reunite with my last ancestor.

I peek at the sky. A falling star shoots – the same one I saw last night. Do stars fall during daytime? Hmmm. Mother would know.

Something snaps gently in my hand, and Meow hisses. When I look again in my passport, on the second page, under my photo, Mother's signature glows with stardust. It has just shown up there as if the falling star had signed it with its tail. Thank you, Mother.

"So, have you got your mother's signature?" Mayor Icelandia de Winter asks when I burst back into her office.

"Yes, ma'am. I do." I show her my signed passport.

"Well, I don't think little girls should travel alone all the way to Rondelia . . . But since you have relatives there, and you know the exact date of the autumn equinox, off you go to Bookrest. And here's your ticket." She hands me a silver Salem-Bookrest Magic Corridor ticket that has my name on it.

When did she get the ticket?

In Salem nobody is allowed to use the Magic Corridors more than once a year, and nobody my age even once. Only adults can use the Magic Corridors. But Mayor Icelandia de Winter says she'll make an exception for me because I'm an orphan and the papyrus letter I told her about indicates I have family in Transcarpathia, or Rondelia.

The mayor leads me to her car. She pours a few lightnings into the engine, and her Salem Thunder convertible starts with a growl.

Mayor Icelandia de Winter warns me that I'm not allowed to know where the Salem-Bookrest Magic Corridor starts. She blindfolds me with a handkerchief, and we're on our way.

We hop on Salem's cobblestones. She honks to scare the kids playing hopscotch in the middle of the street. From the back seat, I listen to Salem's familiar voices. Mrs. Lemonade Jones's daughters chatter about breaking into Mrs. Snippety Smith's chocolaterie at night "to teach that old hag a lesson."

Good luck, I wish Mrs. Lemonade Jones's girls. Next time you can count on me.

I'm still blindfolded when we reach the borders of Salem at the stony Battles Bridge. The warrior witches ask the driver about right of passage.

Mayor Icelandia de Winter whispers something, then they chant with their alto and bass voices, "All is clear at the gates of Salem. It's Mayor Icelandia de Winter. All is clear at the gates of Salem. . ."

After we cross the bridge, I'm out of Salem for the first time in my life. The Ash River murmurs behind me. It's said that since the wars, this river flows in small moaning waves and looks wrinkled like a sad face.

We arrive at the Ghostly-Trees Forest. Mayor Icelandia de Winter helps me out. She leads me through the trees live with a chorus of crickets lamenting that autumn is taking over.

"Don't take off the blindfold until you hear my car leaving," she says when we finally stop. "And good luck to you, Marigold. May the Salem witches be with you."

When the sound of her car fades away, I take off the handkerchief. I hope whatever comes next won't scare me.

I squint, then open my eyes wide: a tall, thick pine tree rises straight in front of me. Suddenly a door takes shape in its trunk and letters pop up one after another:

MAGIC CORRIDOR TO BOOKREST, RONDELIA

My heart thuds as I stare at the letters. But I'm determined. I take a deep breath and thrust my right hand toward the doorknob. The door flies open. A black space spreads in front of me.

Afraid I might have reached the Land of Endless-Night by mistake, I check again the letters on the door. They haven't changed.

Just when I decide to go on, something falls on my head. What is this? I take it off. A woolen shawl tries to jump back on my head and cover my eyes.

How can this be? The only things falling on a witch's head in a forest should be leaves, bugs, and twigs.

There's a roar. An invisible force tosses me on the clover in front of the pine door. My sprawl scares away a few grasshoppers and ladybugs.

Someone laughs, and the forest reverberates sinister echoes. The branches quiver, the nightingales have lost their warbles, and the baby raccoons are hiding in oak and elm hollows.

Above the trees' foliage, a witch whose face is hidden in a silver hood flies on her broom, ready to veer in my direction, her knuckled fingers pointing at me.

A wicked witch? I thought they lived only by the Black Hollow Lake. She snaps some branches, and as she's getting closer, shouts, "Get lost!"

Why should I get lost? I need to travel to Rondelia. Here I go! I jump into the abysmal mouth inside the tree.

As I cross the door jamb, I'm being sucked into a bubble of air. It's like plunging into nothingness -- I'm too amazed to check above my shoulder and see if the wicked witch has followed me.

A strong gust whisks my bubble into the air. It carries me further into the darkness – faster and faster, at light speed. It twists and twirls my air cocoon, while I float in it like a feather. Meow glides all over my T-shirt.

I loop and fall through sucking cascades of black holes and vortex gates that spit me out into the next black corridor with its roller coaster slopes. For a while everywhere is pitch black. It's turned bitterly cold.

Meow sneezes a few times, and I shiver.

A faraway light flashes in front of me. The bubble has taken me to a place with millions of tiny twinkling lights that seem attached like pins to this endless black corridor. They look familiar, like the picture of a nebula I once saw in a catalogue, like a *lion* –

No! I may be from Salem, but this is too much even for a witch apprentice. I mean, is it possible I'm traveling through the galaxy? It's all very confusing, but I have to admit it's likely I'm crossing through constellations, right in the Milky Way. Where else can I be, now that Leo has shown up?

The star-made feline waves its tail under a meteorite palm tree. It roars at Cancer -- which dashes away, clacking its glittery claws, withdrawing behind the shiny horns of Taurus. Virgo walks by my bubble, combing her star hair and chatting with the Gemini about the new season of stardust rain. Now Libra flies above, dropping on each of its star-made weighting pans a silvery fish it got from Pisces. Capricorn sleeps in a field of daisy stars, while Sagittarius shoots an arrow by mistake, I assume, into a black hole.

When Scorpio shows up from behind the Polar Star, wiggling its poisonous tail, Meow hisses at the creature. Ready to sting, Scorpio lashes at me with the venomous tip of its tail.

I push the bubble's walls, trying to make it fly even faster. I dash aimlessly among floating zodiacs, hoping to find a constellation to protect me. Maybe Taurus – it seems so strong.

But before I reach the Bull, the air cocoon hits a meteorite and falls on a pile of seashell stars, near a black hole. It's the very hole Sagittarius shot earlier.

My sprawl attracts the ire of the hollow's lawful resident. A comet squints at me. Swishing, it smashes into the bubble, trying to get to me.

Translucent star glitter covers my bubble. I can hardly see outside but I can hear the comet pounding. How long can these walls last?

There's a crack, then the cocoon fizzles, rolling back.

Next thing, I'm falling in the darned black hole. . . .

Dropping into the abyss, going nowhere, falling, falling, falling. By the Salem witches' wands! Will I crash?

A shooting star that smells of coriander – Mother's scent – emerges from some dark galactic corner and catches my exploding bubble on its long tail.

I fall asleep covered in stardust, carried further into the galaxy, dreaming that my mother holds me in her arms.

2. Theater of Vaudeville

"*I* don't see her fangs," a hoarse voice says.

Two masked faces glare at me. Where am I?

"Look, she's waking up," the other voice says, sounding like a crow's. "Told you she's not dead."

"Yet!" the first voice says. Then to me, "Listen here, girl, why don't you tell us your name?"

I try, but I'm too exhausted to open my mouth. Why does my head hurt? I touch my forehead and find a lump, solid, like a knuckle. The blows from the comet come back to me – and the Scorpio!

I'm lying on a cobblestone street behind a cherry tree that sprinkles little pink flowers over my head. Could this be Bookrest?

"C'mon! Tell us." The two shake me. Never mind that I'm just a little girl, or that, well, it's not polite to treat foreigners like this.

I pull myself together and get shakily to my feet. My backpack is burst open, and all my bandanas, my "I ? Salem" T-shirt, and Mother's seashell are lying on the cobblestones. And I have a teacup-size hole in my jeans, right on my left knee. What a mess! As for Meow, rolled on her back, she's still knocked out.

Finally, I dare look at them. The two are dressed in black trenchcoats, their heads concealed behind raised collars and drooping hat brims. Two pairs of hollow eyes burn, and --

That smell! It resembles the acrid stink the hooded, bug-like creature from Salem oozed. I want to cover my nose, but Meow wakes up, sneezing.

"You're coming with us," the voice on my left says, clasping dark hands around my shoulders. "Or maybe you to want to die right now."

"Die? Excuse me, I am Mari -- "

"Don't play smart with me now, " the creature with the crow voice says. "It's curfew."

My watch with dandelion numbers shows 8:00 p.m.

"I'm sorry. I didn't know," I say, tired and confused, blinking in the hostile moonlight.

"What orphanage did you escape from?" the creature on my right says.

"Or is it the Prison of Tears?" the other one asks, its eyes coals of fire.

By the time their foul smell turns into a nauseating breeze, I decide it's better to keep silent. Maybe I'll have to protect Meow. As for me –

"What's the matter, girl? Cat got your tongue?" the voice on my left says, chuckling, pointing at Meow.

"All right, then. We're going to cut off your tongue," the other voice says. Then to his companion, "C'mon, pull her by the legs. I'll hold her arms."

"We'll teach you a lesson," the creature on my left says, glaring at me.

The two jump over me, squishing Meow. They hold me down on the cobblestones, at the base of the beautiful cherry tree. One of them pulls a giant scissors from a large bag filled with tools: screwdrivers, hammers, and scalpels one of them pulls a giant pair of scissors. The sight of it shining with a morbid luster in the moonlight is terrifying.

"Help! Somebody, please, help me!" I yell from the bottom of my witch lungs. Are these horrible creatures really going to cut off my tongue? Mother –

The faceless attacker on my left opens my mouth, and my body quakes, I try to swallow my tongue but choke and convulse. A star hurtles across the sky. Is it you, Mother? Everything grows dark.

I dream that I'm still wandering through the Milky Way galaxy, that furious Scorpio is still chasing me. But what was the falling star that carried me all the way to this far end of the world? Could it be Mother? Somehow, from the stars above, she might be with me. Right now.

Still terrified, I squint into the night. The creatures in black have gone. Now a kid stares at me, checking my jeans' pockets, rummaging through my knapsack. The moon frames his head like a halo.

Am I dead?

"Wake up!" the boy says. He's grinning, and I can see fangs that gleam.

A wolf boy? But where are his wolf paws and tail? I bite gently the tip of my tongue. By the Salem witches' wands! It's intact.

"Are you coming?" the kid says.

All right! I jump to my feet. Kids smirking between little pearly fangs surround me. Ash covers their faces. They're dressed in patched linen trousers, cotton coats missing sleeves, brimless caps, unlaced boots.

I don't dare ask them about their fangs. I'm just grateful that they look friendly.

The street is dark, like a sad story. Even the moonlight flowing over the cobblestones and the cherry trees loses its glow to the damp air.

"Is this Bookrest?" I ask at last.

"Precisely," the kid who addressed me first says with a lively voice. "By the way, I'm Red. Who're you?"

"I'm Marigold," I say. I throw my things back into my pack and caress a distressed Meow.

"All right, Marigold, it's time to move on," Red says. "How many Black Suits patrols do you think I can fight to save you?" He points in an unknown direction, then thrusts his left hand toward me, as if saying "C'mon!"

I follow him in silence, staring at the gloomy buildings made of falling bricks, shrouded in fog. With the other two kids close behind me, we take the first narrow street to the left of the cherry tree, followed by a trail of alley cats.

I'm too exhausted to run but can still drag behind Red, who walks and jumps over puddles hidden in missing cobblestones.

What is going to happen to me now? And why didn't the Atlas say anything about the faceless creatures with scissors and the wolf boys from Rondelia?

"What orphanage are you from?" Red asks me all of a sudden.

"Excuse me?"

"What's the matter? Don't tell me your mother let you stay out this late." Red shakes a few drops of dew from a cherry leaf into his hands, then washes his face.

By the Salem witches' wands! What is he talking about?

"And where are your fangs?" he asks, staring at my mouth.

I say, "Listen, Mr. Red -- "

"Red will do."

"Red, then. I'm not from here. I'm from Salem."

"Oh, yeah? And I'm from the moon," he says, chuckling.

The other two laugh with him.

What poor manners people have here! I should inform Mr. Londinium Oxford about these rude wolf boys. Or maybe

Mayor Icelandia de Winter can freeze them for an hour with her blizzard and teach them a lesson.

Before I get a chance to ask Red what's so funny, a poodle leaps in front of me. He prances nervously at my feet.

"My companion, Waltz," Red says.

"Waltz, a dog?" I say.

"You bet," the poodle says, waggling his tail.

Maybe I am hallucinating that I'm back in Salem, where witches can -- but only when there's a deadly danger -- give voice to creatures, to listen to their wishes and learn the forest's secrets. Or is this another one of Red's jokes?

"Excuse me, who said that?" I ask.

"I did," the dog says. Then it barks, as if to show me he can do that, too.

I gape at Waltz, while Meow glides from my shoulder onto my belly, making a noise that's part growl, part purr. Waltz is some poodle. His left ear covers his left eye, his right ear stands erect, continuously alert, and his light gray fur, clean but uncombed, is quite a mess.

He stares at my hand, woofs, and asks, "What's with your palm?"

"Just a scrape from the cobblestones, from when I landed here – "

"Show it to me," he says.

I offer Waltz my ripped palm, which is still oozing a few drops of blood.

Waltz licks it twice with his little warm tongue.

By the Salem witches' wand! My wound fades slowly, then disappears.

I want to thank Waltz, but something tickles my palm again. Three shiny lines, which all true Salem witches have hidden on their hands, just appeared in my palm. The silver lifeline crosses it horizontally, the vertical golden health line cuts it like a cross, and from the base of my pinkie down to the thumb the diagonal jade-green magical line gleams, my herbs witch line.

But why did they show up now? I'm not a witch yet.

We've reached an old building made of scarlet-brown bricks. A gang of alley cats swarms around garbage cans, digging holes around the cobblestones, pouncing on roofs. They peek at us and hiss back at Meow, whose hair stretches all over my T-shirt.

"The Theater of Vaudeville," Red says, pointing. "It's where you said you wanted to go – "

The papyrus, Dr. L. Acua, my relative, Mother – they circle in my head like a carousel.

"Hurry! Get in!" Red is practically yelling.

For a second, blinded by the streetlamp light, I lose myself in his aquamarine eyes.

"Are you leaving?" I feel panicky.

"Sorry. I didn't have it planned to rescue you tonight," he says. "What was your name?"

"Marigold."

"Right! Well then, take care. This is no city for lost princesses like you." He winks at the other two kids.

Who does he think he is? Me? A princess? If only he knew that I'm the daughter of the Grand Herbs Witch of Salem. That's it! I want to tell him, but it's too late.

"Goodbye, Marigold of Salemmm. . ." Red's voice fades, and the three vanish in a cloud of fog as big as my wonder about this city, its frightening creatures and wolf boys.

Meow stares at me, her whiskers twitching, while I tremble in anger like a black-cats witch.

Fine! At least if this is the right meeting place according to the papyrus, I'll have no problem finding Dr. L. Acua and my relative. Then my voyage to this land of fog and fright will come to an end before the autumn equinox, before the end of the Harvest Holiday, before fifth grade starts in the Twisted-Wand District.

I walk into a dim hallway ending in a steep staircase that goes down and down, into the unknown. Whom can I ask for a ticket?

The moonlight filtering through a cracked window throws dancing shadows on the walls. Voices resonate from downstairs, and my foot hesitates.

I take the steps slowly. My right hand on the cold metallic banister raises goosebumps. The staircase goes on and on, spiraling all the way down, like a snail that keeps growing. Another step, and another, and another.

The underground hall stretches some twenty feet below street level. It's a dark room with a small stage. I hear chatter and whispers everywhere and sense figure around me, although I can't distinguish their ghostly faces.

Before I can reach a seat, the music of flutes and tambourines spreads in the hall. A dancer shows up, swaying to the cadence of this mysterious song. An opal-blue dress of shimmering veils glides over her body, her coal-black hair falls down her shoulders. She looks beautiful and dangerous, like no witch I've ever seen in Salem.

The dancer leans over a wicker basket and takes out a creature with metallic scales and gleaming eyes.

A python!

Meow has taken refuge on the back of my T-shirt.

The reptile coils around the woman's body, head moving toward her left leg, tail tightening around her neck. To the rhythm of drums, the snake enchantress spins until she turns into a tornado of veils that engulfs both dancer and snake.

For a while she seems lost in that bewitched cocoon. When she reemerges she looks different, like a creature made of flesh and scales.

I blink and tremble. Should I get out of here?

The creature grins, showing two deadly fangs.

By the Salem witches' wands! A vampire.

The audience stands mute and frozen like statues.

Mouth wide open, the vampire leaps into the hall, two steps away from me. She bites an unsuspecting spectator dressed in black who looks like my terrifying assailants with scissors.

I shudder, my courage lost in my stomach. It's a long way out, and the creature is surely faster than I am.

The vampire whispers with a sorceress's voice into its ear. "That's for killing the postmaster." Again she bites her victim, and again, until she makes sure it's dead.

She glares at me, and I feel I'm already dead. But instead of biting me, the vampire grins, showing me her dreadful fangs. After which she moves back to the stage, twisting and spreading veils and scales, until she reassumes the shape of a woman. Then she grabs her python and vanishes behind the red curtains.

The audience awakens, as if from a deadly sleep, yawning and stretching.

Were they hypnotized – or was I?

A scary song with howls resembling the wicked witches' hymn resonates throughout the theater. By the Salem witches' wands! What if the theater is the place where the wicked witches gather?

Right when I put my foot on the stairs, ready to flee, a silhouette takes shape from the steam that has engulfed the stage.

Is this a magician?

He's tall yet skinny like a scarecrow, and his bald skin is white, like chalk. Blood-red lips cut his elongated face gathered around a gargoyle nose, pointed ears, and a sharp chin.

Fluttering like a pair of wings, a black bat-embroidered cape resembling the cloaks from the Salem Museum of Sorcery completes the lurid apparition.

When, eyes closed, the magician raises his arms and opens his mantle, his cape's red satin lining strikes me with horror. Fresh blood is splashed all over it, trickling on the stage and even the hall floor.

The music stops. The creature opens his eyes. The scariest phosphorescent eyes glare at us over a grinning mouth that reveals long yellowish fangs: vampire fangs.

The temperature drops to two icicles – about as cold as when the first blanket of snow covers Salem. Steam comes out of my mouth. Everybody's teeth chatter.

Now the magician's cloak is covered with crawling live bats – all the bat embroidery on that mantle has come to life.

And I don't like bats! I duck to avoid the ghastly creatures.

Aarrgh. The magician fetches one bat by the wings and bites off its head. The panicky audience jumps over rows of seats but only end up stumbling on each other's feet in a stampede.

I'm ahead of the frenzied bunch, trying to flee, when something draws my attention.

Several bats land on the shoulders of a few spectators dressed in black who look like the one the snake enchantress bit to death. The bats pierce their necks while they try in vain to get rid of the little bloodsuckers.

A smell of blood spreads throughout the theater. I touch my neck, terrified that I might end up under the bats' fangs. I'm not hurt, but vampire bats are swarming around me -- I'm right in their midst!

After a few moments of pandemonium that leave three victims in black lying dead on the floor, five children with fangs who look like Red and his companions show up from behind the stage and carry out the corpses.

And there's no trace of the magician or his bats.

What's going on here? Maybe the magician's bats aren't real – they're just one of his tricks. Or maybe the magician has an arrangement with the creatures in black to play the farce of dying under the bats' fangs every night.

Although I can't explain how the dancer could turn into a vampire, then back to a woman, I'm too exhausted after my travel through the Milky Way galaxy to think about it. And the knuckle on my head still hurts.

All this may be sheer fantasy, and I the victim of some hallucination.

A strange hiss behind me reveals my cruel reality. I'm staring into the snake enchantress's face. Her mouth is open wide enough for me to see her glowing fangs.

"Hello, I'm Zelda."

I'm unable to utter a word.

"Come with me," Zelda says.

I want to run away – although I'd also like to ask her about Dr. L. Acua before she bites me.

But the vampire is quicker. She grabs my hand and drags me through a narrow maze-like corridor all the way to her backstage room. She pushes me into a small dressing room whose walls are covered with cracked round, square, and oblong mirrors.

Although I should be scared, I decide to stand brave like a true Salem herbs witch.

"Listen," she says. "The Black Suits have tracked you down. They know you've come here to find Dr. L. Acua." She combs her hair with a large seashell and dresses up in a robe made of silver snake scales.

"Excuse me, is Dr. L. Acua here?" I ask with a faint voice. Instead of answering my question she tells me with a glint in her eyes that the Black Suits went to the post office and tortured the postmaster.

"Poor fellow, he died confessing he sent Dr. L. Acua's letter to you."

I take a seat on an ivory chair, far away from the wicker basket where the scary python's forked tongue zips in and out in Meow's direction. My gliding T-shirt cat meows desperately – I'd better change my shirt before I drive her mad.

Zelda tells me that the people in this country are preparing to overthrow its cruel rulers, "the Black Suits and their leader, the Black Bug."

Of course I immediately think of the bug-like creature back in Salem and the smelly, faceless ones from Bookrest.

Zelda says these thugs have governed Rondelia for the past fifty years. They put rebels in prison and kill people every day. "We're Gonna Get You!" is their motto."

And when night falls, the Black Suits break into people's homes and snatch their children, whom they put into orphanages with the purpose of raising them as a new generation of loyal Black Suits.

The Black Suits have banned, burned, or shredded all the books that can bring dreams and hope to the people. They've killed the fairies and the witches, the tales and the legends. They've razed forests and polluted the rivers.

"They've killed the past," Zelda says, her eyes turning black.

She stops to drink from a glass filled with pansies floating on a blue liquid, then offers me some "pansy cider." It tastes sweet-and-sour, like Mrs. Lemonade Jones's anti-shyness boost Mother made me drink last summer until I got sick to my stomach.

Zelda says the Black Suits have forced the people to dress in gray. They've banned all colors. In their cruel wisdom, they've declared sadness and scarcity the ruling principles of their society.

"Worse still, they've left us without a future," she says. "You see, the future is made of people's hopes. But no one in Rondelia dares hope any longer."

The weirdest part of all is that nobody has ever seen the Black Suits' leader. People call him the Black Bug on account of the Black Suits' bug-like appearance. "Some think he's a dragon, others say he's a vampire. But Dr. L. Acua would've known him, he would've told us. Definitely not a vampire."

Others think the Black Bug simply doesn't exist, that he's just a rumor the Black Suits have spread to keep the population terrified.

I feel saddened about the world I find here. Yet as I listen to Zelda's words, a wicked little thought raises a smirk on my face: Wouldn't it be great to send Mrs. Snippety Smith to the Black Suits and free all the chocolates of Salem?

"And now," she says, interrupting my spiteful chocolate fantasy, her eyes glowing, "we're going to meet with Dracula."

"What are you talking about? You mean Dracula as in D-r-a-c-u-l-a?" I feel weak, like I'm made of water. Meow hisses. Wasn't I supposed to meet Dr. L. Acua? The papyrus said. . ."Excuse me -- "

Zelda's glare freezes my words on my lips.

I'm cold again. I can't keep my body from shaking. After all, my world is a world of nice Salem witches, not of vampires. I don't like vampires! Maybe I can stand a vampire or two, like Zelda and even the magician with his bats. But not Dracula. Dracula is scary, and dangerous, and deadly.

The lights around me fade out. It's suddenly getting dark. I want my mother.

I feel drops of water being sprinkled on my face. I wake up to an unknown red room.

"Finally," the woman says.

I remember. I'm in Bookrest, she's Zelda the vampire, and I'm about to meet Dracula! I wish I'd never found the papyrus letter, never left Salem. No Black Suits. No vampires. At the end of September I'd have started fifth grade. That simple.

We're moving along in the same dim maze-shaped corridor. I'm praying that Dracula has no grudge against little Salem witches like me.

My eyes are fixed on the ceiling. The bulbs aren't real bulbs – they're neither magic talking bulbs like we have back home nor are they electricity bulbs like the kind they have in the cities of skyscrapers. No, these bulbs are filled with swarming fireflies. And because some have more fireflies than others, their light ranges from bright to obscure.

Just when a firefly-loaded bulb explodes behind me, freeing all the little luminescent insects inside, we reach a door on which is written in blood-red:

THE MAGICIAN

Great! The magician's performance with his bats, the freezing temperature, and the smell of crypt suddenly come to my mind. I want to turn back, but Zelda holds my hand in a fierce clutch.

"Courage!" she says, pushing the magician's door open.

That creepy cemetery-and-mushrooms odor hits me again. As my eyes get used to the dark light, lines of bats hanging on the walls like ornaments show up from the mist.

Something quivers in the back of the room. A cadaverous white hand appears right in front of me. The nails are so sharp, pointed, and yellowish that I close my eyes, wishing everything around me were just a bad dream. But a second corpse-like hand thrusts itself at me, and soon these hands twist together as if dancing, trying to hypnotize me. At last, when the magician's head comes out of the darkness and peers straight into my eyes – scaring Meow, who faints on my left sleeve – my stomach shrinks and my knees threaten to abandon me for good.

"Hello." The magician's voice is cavernous. "I am Prince Drrracula."

My face is hot. I try to say something. I stumble, stagger, regain balance, finally babble something unintelligible that might possibly count as a greeting. Who would have thought to find Dracula at the call of a papyrus letter signed by –

Then it hits me.

Dr. L. Acua. That's it! Connect and invert the letters from the signature, and D-r-L-A-c-u-a becomes D-R-A-C-U-L-A.

A strange mix of anxiety and euphoria overwhelms me.

"I have to attend to my snake," Zelda says. "But hurry now! With four Black Suits down, more are surely are on their way." With that she walks out of the room.

I am left alone with Dracula.

"As I was saying," the magician says, "I am Prince Dracula."

I take an official position like I would in front of Mayor Icelandia de Winter -- shoulders back, head up, face serious – and say in one breath, "Hello my name is Marigold. I am the last herbs witch of Salem and I've come to Bookrest to find my relative from Transcarpathia."

"Ah, that!" Dracula says. "I was expecting someone else -- not you, not a little girl."

"My mother, maybe?" I dare say. "She's. . .dead."

A shadow crosses Dracula's face. His eyebrows draw into a sinister V-shape, and his fangs glitter over his long, sharp, incredibly red tongue.

Dracula falters as I reveal to him how Mother disintegrated into green dust. As soon as I'm done telling him how the muddy bug-like creature melted upon touching the red dragon seal, he drags his cloaked body into the faint light and drops in an upholstered red leather armchair with a plop.

He sips from a blood-red liquid that bubbles in a tall tubular glass. I don't dare ask what the strange drink might be, but one thing is sure: no pansies float in it.

Dracula offers me a seat on a black divan with dozens of red pillows. He walks to the back of the room, where he takes off his blood-soaked cloak. Under it, he wears a black T-shirt with the head of a scarlet dragon. His tattered black leather trousers are two inches short, leaving in plain view his unusually long legs shoved into black cowboy boots.

"Call me Mr. D," he says, then he dons on a new black satin cape and a black fedora. "It's shorter, easier, and I like it more than Dracula. After all, this is the twentieth century." He says he has some secrets to confide in me. "But only if you promise not to share them with anybody."

"Sure," I say. Who in my class would ever believe me if I were to tell them I've met Dracula?

In a conspiratorial voice, Mr. D tells me he's organizing the Underground, a group made up of vampire kids, Roma magicians, and others who work at overturning the Black Suits.

"You're a Salem witch, aren't you?" he says.

"Not yet. I will be when I reach thirteen and pass the Witchcraft Test. Until then I'm just a girl."

"And a brave one, by the looks of it."

I stare, undecided. I guess "nerd witch" doesn't stand for courage.

"Tell you what," Mr. D says, "if you give me a helping hand with the Underground, I promise I'll help you find your relative. I swear to you on my Halloween birthday."

Halloween! Back home we lock our doors on Halloween. It's the night when the wicked witches hunt the good witches of Salem. It's the night when winds unleash their full fury, tugging trees upside-down, their roots stretching in the air like octopuses' arms. It's the night when, riding on their brooms, the bad witches cross the moon from right to left and left to right, trying to make it dizzy, and fall on our roofs.

Mr. D picks up on my hesitation. "I'm very sick," he says. "My gums hurt, and my fangs keep aching and shaking." For years the Black Suits have kept him in the Prison of Tears. They've used horrible machines with tubes, electricity, and cuffs to drain many of his powers. He can't levitate, can't turn into a bat or a werewolf, but can still climb the walls like a lizard. "And of course, I still govern all the vampires in the world," he says, puffing up.

Agile as a cat, he snatches an unsuspecting bat asleep on the wall and bites off the doomed creature's head.

Yuck. I want to turn around. But how can I offend Mr. D by showing how disgusting I find his eating habits?

As for sucking blood, Mr. D says that when the Black Suits took over, he decided he was going to help the Rondelians. He preys only on Black Suits and their thug allies. Zelda and his other vampire friends are doing the same. "No women, no kids, no innocent people!"

I still haven't made up my mind to join the Underground. True, the call comes from the great Dracula. True, he hasn't bitten me yet.

"Excuse me," I say, "why did you call Mother here before the autumn equinox?"

"Ah, that!" Mr. D says. "I'm sure your relative from Transcarpathia will be able to answer all your questions." As he finishes off the bat, he smears blood all over his face.

"But Mr. D, that's why I can't help you, don't you see?" I say. "If I were to join the Underground, I'd lose my relative." I remind Mr. D that it's already Saturday night, and that my last ancestor will perish when autumn arrives next Saturday, on September twenty-first. "You said so in your letter. That's why I need to go to Transcarpathia first."

"Marigold, that's exactly where I'm going now – to Transcarpathia, to my Castle Bran," Mr. D says with a glorious voice. "I forgot my lyre there, about half a century ago, and that was no ordinary instrument."

For some reason, enthusiasm overwhelms me.

"Great!" Mr. D says, seeing the sparkle in my eyes. "Then it's a deal."

He wants to shake on it, but glancing from my tiny palm to his huge hand, he offers me his pinkie's fingertip, which I clasp with both hands and pump vigorously.

And so I, Marigold -- the last herbs witch of Salem, shake hands with the great Dracula of Transcarpathia, who sits one foot away from me and who's taking me to my last living relative, now that I have nobody left and Mother has turned into a falling star.

3. The Vampire Kids

$\mathcal{M}$r. $\mathcal{D}$ changes the contours of his body and arches like a bow. He places his limbs on the floor, his hands turn into paws, and his ears grow like a bat's.

He creeps around the room, but he doesn't look like a vampire any more, nor does he look like a lizard – he looks like both! In spite of all these transformations, his eyes are the same: big, hollow-looking, and sad.

"Why don't you hop on my back, and we'll be at Castle Bran in no time," Mr. D says.

My head still hurts from the recent attacks and feels a little swimmy from the latest extraordinary events taking place in my life at such a fast pace. But I've enough energy left to fetch my knapsack and climb on his back. Before I know it, we're out in the alley cats' street.

The city is silent and misty. The moon crowns the star-spattered sky, throwing a soft light on Mr. D's lizard scales. He gallops faster and faster, sometimes avoiding a frightened cat, sometimes leaping over a puddle of water quivering where a cobblestone is missing.

On his back, I clasp his body tightly – it's my only chance to survive this race to Transcarpathia.

All of a sudden Mr. D stops and focuses in the depths of the night. "Black Suits!" he yells.

They're waiting for us. Two dozen Black Suits -- all dressed up with black trenchcoats and masks, and with faceless burning eyes -- send their rotten smell toward us. I take it the offensive begins with a direct assault on our noses.

Mr. D's roar sounds like a wolf's. Mouth elongated into a muzzle, fangs sticking out, skin that looks like an armor of iron scales – he's ready to attack. Here is Dracula in his grandeur, the real vampire, not the magician from the Theater of Vaudeville. By the Salem witches' wands! I hope I never make him angry.

"Give up!" one Black Suit yells at us with a crow's voice.

"Come and get me!" Mr. D roars back. Then toward me, whispering, "Gee, Marigold, that darn fang ache is back. I need your help."

"What should I do?"

"Yell 'Red.'"

"What?" I say, my eyes whirlpools of wonder.

"Red's my assistant. He'll show up with the V-kids."

Is he talking about the wolf boys? "V-kids?" I ask, breathless.

"Yes, vampire children."

Vampires? The knuckle on my head sends a pang into my body.

"Arghhh, the fang!" Mr. D cries, holding his swollen cheek.

I stand frozen at the thought that I've been only in the company of deadly vampires and Black Suits from the very moment I set foot in Bookrest. And I thought the Land of Endless-Night was the deadliest place on earth –

The Black Suits unleash their attack. But they don't just run, they run-glide, like mollusks. They jump over Mr. D, throwing him to the ground.

"Red!" I yell. I duck as a Black Suit thrusts its hand toward my throat. I run in all directions, like a scared rabbit, hoping that Mr. D can keep them busy. And so he does.

The Black Suits stick Mr. D to the cobblestones. They smash fists into his body. But Mr. D never yells. Instead, he waits for the Black Suits to come close to his face – one at a time – and bites their necks, making a precise incision in the carotid. His eyes sparkling, Mr. D sucks their blood and licks his lips.

He's up again, throwing the dozen corpses away like bowling pins.

"Red!" I yell, encouraged.

Another dozen Black Suits attacks Mr. D. But this time they're careful not to approach his deadly fangs.

Then catastrophe strikes. All of a sudden, Mr. D jerks and releases a long howl. I take it it's the fang. I don't know how serious it is, but by the looks of a collapsing Mr. D, that tooth is beyond shaking.

Still Mr. D fights and bites, no matter how many lashes, bullets, and bayonets the Black Suits thrash, shoot, or stab into his body – until he falls like a rock, wailing. The Black Suits chain and cuff him. Mr. D is still enjoying a bite or two, which keeps the Black Suits busy, so they forget about me.

Oh, no! If they take Mr. D away, how am I going to reach Transcarpathia?

As I'm struggling to find a hiding place – maybe behind some lampposts – the earth beneath my green shoes shakes vigorously. Through the two holes of a sewer lid, two eyes stare at me.

"Did you call me?" a voice asks.

"Red?"

"Yep! Get in," the vampire kid says. "Quick!"

He pulls the lid away, and down I go into the darkness.

"Don't worry, the Black Suits won't get down here. They're no match for our vampire bites."

Red's eyes and pearly fangs shine ghastly in the moonlight. By now a vampire's proximity doesn't scare me any more – even Meow has gotten used to it.

"You again?" Red asks, staring at me.

I blush, hoping this time he'll show some manners. After all, he rescued me – twice.

"Marigold, is that right? I didn't think you'd need my help again – and during the same night," he says, pointing into the darkness.

"Where are you taking me now?"

"Into my world, beneath the streets of Bookrest, to the underground city of vampire children."

I gulp. Back in Salem, the wicked witches haunt the catacombs by the Black Hollow Lake. Nobody dares go down there. Not even Mother would go. They say Mrs. Snippety Smith once tried to search for her missing daughter in the catacombs because the wicked witches snatched her little girl's soul.

But when she got there, the evil witches scared her badly, even tried to kill her. Barking like mad dogs, they chased Mrs. Snippety Smith through tunnels filled with corpses and skeletons. They yelled that they were going to snatch her soul and dress in her body afterward.

Eventually Mrs. Snippety Smith escaped from the catacombs, but she never recovered. She turned ugly and bad like a wicked witch. And from that day on, she hated little girls like me.

But I've always felt sorry for Mrs. Snippety Smith – except when it comes to chocolate, which is where our major disagreement begins. Hmmm, did Mrs. Lemonade Jones's daughters make it into Mrs. Snippety Smith's chocolaterie the night I left Salem?

"What about Mr. D?" I ask Red.

He says we can't do anything about it, that he's used to rescuing Mr. D from wherever the Black Suits might take him. "It'll take a while until we track him down. Surely we'll have to fight the Black Suits. And that's something only us, vampire kids, can do!"

We're strolling under the surface of the city. The moon reflects strange lights through the sewer lids' holes and onto the soggy tunnels. It's like walking through a curtain made of uneven rays of violet light.

I imagine all sorts of horrible things the Black Suits might use on Mr. D – boiling water, pikes, scaffolds. I'm disheartened by how quickly my quest in Rondelia has come to a dead end.

We've reached the depths of the city, some thirty feet below street level. Clouds of steam swirl around us, lifting through the sewers and up into the now eerily silent streets.

When the mist has slowly dissipated and my eyes have adjusted to the darkness, a cool breeze touches my body.

At an invisible command, a few candles stuck in the cave's walls light up one after another. They form a flickering path that punctures the darkness around. The orange light from the candles strikes the brown walls, which seem restful to my eyes.

An entire network of tunnels winds away in every direction. Red says we're taking the northern tunnel.

By now I've had some time to observe him. Red must be about my age. Unlike the others I've seen, he's dressed in a school uniform: black jacket and trousers, a white shirt. Like me, he's pug-nosed. Red wears his dark-blond hair in a short cut, a few wisps falling above his intense eyes.

Red notices my curiosity. He's an orphan, he says. Two years ago he ran away.

"I waited until the orphanage guards went off to bed and jimmied the lock on the dormitory's window." He jumped down to the courtyard and ran. He hid behind trees, crept in the grass, crawled through shrubs, bushes, and underbrush until he reached the woods. Exhausted, he stopped to eat some wild blackberries – and heard orphanage guards yelling and dogs barking.

"I knew they'd chase me like a rabbit and kill me if they found me." He started running again, but his body was too weak from lack of proper food and from beatings. He stumbled on a rock, fell down a ravine, and broke his left leg. He could still crawl in the darkness, but the voices and the barking behind him only got louder. "I prayed I'd be killed quickly, without pain. But I also wished I'd met my mother before I died."

He saw a big shadowy figure jumping from a tree in front of him. His heart stopped – he thought the terror and the pain from the broken leg were making him hallucinate. But the shadow was none other than Mr. D, who grabbed Red and fled, saving his life.

"That's when Mr. D gave me vampire powers," Red says.

Vampire powers? Does he mean Mr. D bit him?

"Mr. D adopted me, and now I'm his assistant." His voice rises. "I rule over the sewers of Bookrest. And last Sunday was my birthday. I'm twelve now, which means I've become a real man, actually. A gentle-man."

He giggles and leaps as if playing imaginary hopscotch right in the stream trickling on the cave's soggy ground.

Hmmm. Red has a self-confident attitude, and there's something elegant in the way he walks – balanced, like an actor. Not like me, a scared mouse!

"You know, I also lost my mother," I say softly.

"I'm sorry," Red says. "How did it happen?"

"Mother turned into a falling star. She was a Salem herbs witch."

"Your mother was a witch?" Red's eyes sparkle. "Then are you a witch too?"

"Yes, we're good Salem witches. But I'm just a girl now," I say. "I've three more years to become a witch. I have to pass a Witchcraft Test, and then. . . "

"But how come witches die?"

"I don't know." I tell Red that Mother's wasn't an ordinary death, according to our doctors, that she was supposed to turn into green sap. "Instead, she disintegrated into green dust."

"How strange," Red says. "And when did this happen?"

"Two days ago." I tell Red how I was coming back from school, bumped into a black bug-shaped creature by my home's gate, found Mother dead and a black footprint near her bed, discovered the papyrus in my attic. How the same bug-shaped creature attacked me and tried to snatch the papyrus from my hand but ultimately melted into a puddle of black mud upon touching the red dragon seal.

A strange thing happens while I'm recounting these events: I see the entire story in a new light. I hesitate.

But Red doesn't. "Don't you think your mother was murdered?"

My face is hot. "I beg your pardon?"

"Your mother was killed," Red says. "Don't you see it?"

By the Salem witches' wands! I thought – hoped – Mother had turned into a falling star, that she had simply died. Murder means violence, pain, suffering. I don't want to think of Mother's death like that.

Right hand in his pocket, Red stares at his black shoes, kicks a pebble into the stream, then says in a low voice, "I'm sure the Black Suits killed your mother."

"What?" I drop my backpack.

"I'm in the Underground. I know things." He says the latest news they got yesterday from Mr. D was how a Black Suit had traveled through a Magic Corridor in search of the last herbs witch of Salem, whom Mr. D had asked to join the Underground. "I suppose it was your mother. We were sure she'd help us blow away those nasty Black Suits."

I stop walking. Wait a minute! Can it be, can it truly be that Mother was . . . murdered? I lean against a soppy wall, stagger, lose balance, and fall on my butt. I cry from the depths of my witch body.

"Motherrrrrr, I will avenge you!" I say between sobs.

"Take it easy now," Red says gently. "In a way, you already did."

"How?" I swallow some tears, bite my nails.

"Because that Black Suit never came back." Red sounds very sure.

I remember the hissing of the creature melting, how it turned into a puddle of mud. "The red dragon seal. . ." I whisper.

"That's right," Red says. "Burned it to death." Red says the seal contained a powerful Roma poison the color of red ink. "It's for Black Suits. It kills them on the spot."

I'm still numb when Red says we've crossed the city on a diagonal and will soon reach the vampire kids' headquarters, which he calls the Cathedral.

It strikes me that Bookrest is about the size of Salem: here, too, everything is within walking distance. The difference is that in Salem we don't walk through tunnels, we fly on brooms.

We reach a glowing niche that opens in the left wall. Invisible hands wash all sorts of small shirts, trousers, and socks, then hang them on lines that appear from nowhere. What kind of magic is this?

"Our spells laundry room," Red says matter-of-factly.

A laundry room with spells? Hmmm. Why not, since back home we wash our clothes with witches' spells? I once tried to explain to a boy from the cities of skyscrapers that in Salem we weave our dresses with special threads twined from grass and leaves, then we glue them with sap and wax, and in the end we sprinkle them with pollen and shell dust. But did he believe me? He did not. So why should I bother to tell Red.

Before I can ask him more about the laundry room, the candles fizzle their short-lived flames and vanish. Although there are no candles around, there's light, just as before. The new illumination comes from a strong source ahead of us – though I can't tell what it is – where the tunnel opens into a cavern.

"That's the Cathedral," Red says.

Wax from who knows how many candles drips down the giant cave's walls. It covers them like Flemish medieval tapestries with knights and dragons Mr. Londinium Oxford showed us once.

Lines of wooden beds carved with bats, dragons, lizards, and wolves are aligned on the left wall.

Halfway through the cave, we meet the vampire kids. They're between the ages of three and fourteen, dressed in colorless rags. The little vampires sense our presence, salute Red, and wave at Waltz. They peer at me mistrustfully.

"The Hawks," Red says, introducing me to V-kids of about nine years old and up, "and the Midgets." He points to the smallest ones.

Reassured, they grin at me, showing their little fangs.

In the back of the grotto lies a giant organ with rusty pipes. But the keyboard seems solid.

"Does anybody play the organ?" I ask Red.

"Nobody," he says. "It's Mr. D's Vampire Organ. He played it for centuries." Red tells me that the organ's music sends a vampire wave, connecting all the vampires in the country. "More than that, the Vampire Organ is one of the greatest inventions of all times."

"Why?"

"Because it's the first combination of magic and technology." Red explains that before the advent of the Vampire Organ, magic and technology were separate. "Magic works with potions, chants, and spells. Technology works with nails, engines, and vaseline. But the organ is both magic and technology."

"Wow!"

Yet when he brought it from Transcarpathia to Bookrest, Mr. D forgot the main piece that made it work: a magic lyre, the key to the Vampire Organ. And since he can't play it these days, the vampire kids are keeping it safe for him. Still Mr. D has vowed to return to Castle Bran and get the lyre back.

"But that's exactly where we were going when the Black Suits attacked us – to Transcarpathia," I say, wondering if Mr. D is still alive – or, well, undead.

"But why would you want to go to Transcarpathia?" Red asks.

"Because I have relatives there."

Red throws me an astonished dark-blue look.

"What's the matter?" I ask.

"You have relatives in Transcarpathia? You?" He frowns at me.

"Yes! That's why I came here all the way from Salem!" Meow nods to back me up.

"And you say you're a witch?" Red looks confused. "But don't you know only vampires live in Transcarpathia?"

I take a seat on a bat-shaped wooden chair next to Red, who sits on a dragon bench. He takes off his school jacket and throws it on a hanger that has shown up from nowhere. When the hanger leaves, a big red brush comes straight for Waltz.

41

Upon reaching his messy fur, the brush starts combing and massaging it, which makes him so happy that he begins to purr, even though he's not a cat.

All of a sudden it strikes me that tranquility reigns in this forgotten place. Even time rests here. It doesn't matter if it's day or night, if it snows or rains or if a furnace-summer heat boils the city on the surface.

"Red," I whisper, "what's with all these vampire children?"

His face suddenly turns serious, his vampire ears erect.

"I didn't mean to offend you, Red – "

"No, it's all right," he says. "Since you too have lost your mother, I'll tell you." He explains to me that many years ago the Black Suits forced every family to give up a child. Apparently they wanted to build an army of loyal children. They stuck the kids in orphanages and tried to erase their home memories and brainwash them into mindless human soldiers.

Of course, the parents refused to give up their children, so at nighttime the Black Suits would raid entire districts and seize all the children they could find. Nobody could do anything to stop them.

Tears fill Red's eyes. "I'm sure my mom is one of those parents." Yet many children ended up in the street, because the orphanage was a horrible experience. They would do everything to escape the beatings, the starvation, and the orphanage guards' abuse. The lucky ones, like Red, came under Mr. D's care.

He would pick them up from wherever he found them – starving on a street corner, shivering in rain or snow, waiting to be chased and killed – and give them the great force of a vampire.

"That's how we all became vampire kids – V-kids, for short."

"Did Mr. D actually bite you?" I ask.

"Yes, but it wasn't that bad." Red sounds as if he's referring to a bee sting. "Would you like to try?" he asks, his little fangs gleaming.

"No! I mean, no thank you. It's not like having a finger pricked, you know." Phew! I pretend I'm searching through my backpack. I avoid Red's gaze, afraid he might get some funny ideas and try his vampire-bite tricks on my neck.

I'm about to ask Red more about the vampire kids when he jumps, dresses back in his magically dry-cleaned school jacket, and says, "Listen, it was nice talking to you, but now I have some unfinished vampire business to attend to – "

"Vampire business?" I ask, afraid I'm going to end up alone again.

"Yep!" He buttons his jacket, throws a jackknife into his right pocket, and raises the collar around his face. He looks mysterious and cocky -- not like any boy I've ever met back in the cities of skyscrapers. "I'm going out with the Hawks, to find Mr. D," he says.

"Now? But it's midnight."

"But don't you worry. Waltz will take care of you."

With that he vanishes into a tunnel, from which his voice echoes, "Bye-bye, Marigold of Salemmm. . ."

Now what? Tired and alone in the world of vampire kids, mostly Midgets, I head for a bed. As I tuck in, the wool blanket seizes me, taking the shape of my body. Waltz jumps in my bed, lies next to me, and purrs along with Meow.

"Good night," he says, licking my face.

It's my first night in this gray forlorn city, not only an ancient place of long-forgotten books but also a sad world of orphans-turned-vampires.

What's this noise? Just when I was dreaming that Mrs. Snippety Smith had finally rescued her daughter from the wicked witches' catacombs.

"Alaaarm!" the Midgets yell, dashing around me. "Alaaarm!"

"Hurry, Marigold," Waltz yelps, his fur standing up like a boar's. "We're under attack."

"From whom?" I jump from my bed.

"Black Suits!" Waltz tells me the Black Suits have started to drill a hole in the Cathedral's ceiling – the closest spot to street level – hoping to snatch out some vampire children. "But they're afraid to get in. They know the V-kids'll finish them off in a heartbeat."

"But I don't understand. The V-kids are just children --."

"With fangs, remember? Not only do they bite to kill, but the Black Suits' deadly poisons don't touch them."

"Really?"

"The Roma spells do the trick," Waltz says. "We're a true army, you know."

And so they are, for now the Midgets polish their fangs, genuflect and stretch their arms, march and align to their right and left in symmetrical pairs, and jump on a rock, blasting it to tiny pieces. Others glue, stretch, and aim slingshots to a faraway target at the back of the Cathedral, smashing pebbles into soup cans and plastic bottles. Still others fight karate-style, yelling "Vampire power!" with true warrior voices.

Waltz and I reach the tallest place in the cavern, where a dozen Midgets climb on each others' shoulders, trying to reach the Cathedral's ceiling.

The cavern trembles, reverberating the drills like thunders, and dust falls over our sleepless faces. Meow spits out a hairball. Waltz coughs.

"What are these kids doing?" I ask Waltz, holding my left hand like a roof above my squinting eyes.

"Welcoming the Black Suits." Waltz says that whenever the Black Suits dig or drill a new hole into the Cathedral's ceiling, the V-kids build up a giant ladder made of their bodies and wait for the Black Suits to show up through the holes. "Then, wham, they bite'em!"

An eyes-burning faceless head shows up through a foot-wide hole, followed by the now well-known Black Suits stench.

The V-kid on the top of the live ladder thrusts his little vampire mouth toward the head. But the Black Suit is quicker and vanishes back through the vertical tunnel and up onto the surface of the city.

Then another Black Suit follows, and another, and another. The children change on the ladder's top position, and each time a Black Suit shows up, another brave little Midget jumps in a ferocious attack.

The V-kids spray Roma magic red ink on the Black Suits, who disappear back in the tunnel with a familiar melting hiss.

"They burn for good," Waltz says, waggling his tail.

By now a bitten Black Suit lies dead on the ground, while the children yell, "Hurray! We're the V-kids with no parents, we'll eat the Black Suits in two seconds!"

All of a sudden a Midget loses balance – his heels slide – and the contraption made of children bounces. Any second, it'll collapse. I leap in their direction and prop its base with my arms and head, with Meow's tail, with Waltz's paws. I push and push – this takes more energy than I thought – and the ladder straightens. The kids holler. The fight is still on.

By the Salem witches' wands! I've just joined the Underground. If only Mother could see me. . . .

The sound of a Black Suit approaching through the tunnel spreads in the Cathedral. The top V-kid opens his mouth, ready for another vampire strike.

But instead of a bug-face, a ball falls through the tunnel from above, missing us by only an inch. It falls to the ground, right in front of me, where it whines.

What's this? The whining ball suddenly sprawls out into a little girl. She must be around eight years old. Chestnut curls cover her round head.

"He-hello, I'm Ro-Rose," she says, dusting at her clothes, "Who're you?"

"I'm Marigold – "

"What's this place, an or-orphanage?" Rose asks.

"This is the Cathedral," Waltz says. Then to me, "We've been waiting for her." He tells me that Mr. D rescued Rose from the Black Suits a week ago in Thriller Books Square. But then they lost track of her. "Maybe Mr. D scared her with his fangs."

Well. Who wouldn't feel her knees melting under the vampire's ferocious glare and morbid fangs?

"I saw the ho-hole," Rose says, "and wanted to play hi-hide and seek in it." She stares at the Midget's ladder, ready to cry at the sight of the V-kids' fangs.

"Don't worry, it's safe here." Then Waltz turns to me. "She's a bit confused now – they all are when they first get here – but she'll be fine in a couple of days." He explains that the transition from human to V-kid makes her dizzy, that the blood changes, and the senses become stronger.

I look at the girl more closely. She doesn't even know that she already has two small fangs, or that her eyes are changing as they blink, the pupils shrinking vertically like a cat's – or, well, like a vampire's.

I leave the V-kids behind to patch the hole with a peculiar mixture that solidifies when spattered on the ceiling. Waltz says it's an old Roma magic mending clay.

Too tired to listen to him, I head for my bed. I hide under the blanket and put on my "I ? Salem" T-shirt – best to give Meow a break.

"Bet you're hungry," Waltz says, pulling the blanket off my head.

We reach the dwarf-size tables in the southern tunnel, in a niche the size of a classroom – the kitchen. Girls with long ink-black hair and wide layered skirts looking like purple petunias in full bloom welcome me.

"These are the Fortune sisters from the Roma spell-caster clan," Waltz says.

"Hello," I say, just before invisible hands around me start peeling oranges, arranging strawberries on jelly cakes, mixing mashed peaches in crystal bowls, pouring lemonade in carafes. Others wash dishes in a foam-filled sink and pop a sheet of chocolate-chip cookies into a silver oven.

By the Salem witches wands! This place smells like all the flavors from the kitchens of Mrs. Baguette Higgins, Mrs. Snippety Smith, and Mrs. Lemonade Jones blended together.

"Waltz, who are these Roma spell-casters?" I ask.

"They're allies, they're not vampires." The Romas, he says, once were powerful magicians. But when the Black Suits came to power they forced them to renounce their magic ways and scattered them all over Rondelia. From that day on, the Romas vowed to take revenge and entered the alliance with the vampires against the Black Suits. And their magic spells have made the vampire kids resistant not only to Black Suits' poisons but also to sunlight.

"V-kids," Waltz says, "are the only vampires in the world who can stand sun. Unlike Mr. D."

"What do you mean?"

"Mr. D is the strongest vampire in the world. Because of that no spells can kill him – or shield him. Not even Roma spells. That's why he likes the moon and gets out only after sunset and before sunrise."

"What about the Fortunes?" I take a seat opposite Rose, who's now drinking a strawberry smoothie.

"The Fortunes are the V-kids' protectors, their godmothers." Waltz says. "They attend the Cathedral and use Roma magic to feed the V-kids and wash their clothes. And in case you're interested, this is Red's personal arrangement with Zaraza the Roma spell-caster, the V-kids' matron, and Mr. D's girlfriend."

I'm shocked at the thought that Mr. D – a vampire, the undead – has a girlfriend. But then, why not? In the end, I have to accept that Mr. D is as real a creature as any Salem witch who can love and hate.

"Zaraza looks twenty but she's a hundred and twenty," Waltz says. "It's said that she keeps her body and face young with the help of spells, that she's the sister of none other than Zelda. Zelda and Zaraza are half-human half-spirit, half-woman half-snake, half-Roma half-magician."

Wow! Maybe I'll get a chance to meet the Roma spell-casters and see what kind of magic they use, what guilds they belong to, whether they talk to cats, or fly on brooms.

"As for Zelda – I know you met her at the Theater of Vaudeville – Mr. D saved her from the Black Suits' dungeons during a terrible thunderstorm night." Waltz flicks the cartilage of his bone supper. "She was so badly wounded, she'd have died if Mr. D hadn't brought her back to afterlife. On that night, Zelda swore to help Mr. D fight the Black Suits."

A holler from the northern tunnel resonates throughout the Cathedral.

"We've found Mr. D!" Red yells, storming in, gathering all the vampire children around him. He says that since the Black Suits took Mr. D away, the Hawks spread all over Bookrest. They spied on the Black Suits, peeped through doors, and listened under open windows. They followed the Black Suits in the streets, ducked behind street lamps and cherry trees, even went so far as to hide under tables in diners to listen to Black Suit conversations. "And we haven't lost anyone!"

It seems that in the afternoon, a group of five Hawks spotted an unusual truck made entirely of stainless steel and locked with seven seals. They followed it on their bikes until the truck stopped at the terrible orphanage from which Red had escaped a few years ago. They spied and saw Mr. D handcuffed inside. And they heard a Black Suit say that since the Prison of Tears was filled with parents looking for their kids, there'd been nowhere else to take the captive vampire but to the orphanage.

"And that's where we're heading now," Zelda says, showing up at the end of the Hawks' battalion.

What a relief! At least they haven't killed Mr. D.

Red and the V-kids gear up with knives, bats, and slingshots. Some put on an eye patch, like a pirate's, others rub ash over their bodies for camouflage. I join in the frenzy and tear off my jeans over both of my kneecaps so I'll look rugged, ready for battle. Red gives me stones to distribute to the V-kids for the slingshots.

I hurry to grab the knapsack I left on my bed – only to find Rose rummaging through it like a little thief. What on earth is she doing?

"Do you have a picture of your mo-mother?" she says.

"Is that what you're looking for?"

"I want to see how a mother lo-looks," she says. "I've ne-never seen one – I don't remember mi-mine and neither do the kids from the orphanage."

"I don't carry a portrait of Mother with me – but I do have her magic shell," I say, turning my backpack upside down and combing through pink, red, and orange bandanas.

While I'm holding it in my hand, the shell suddenly warms up, radiating a strange blue light, like some sort of photographic projection.

Rose moves her little pudgy body near mine to glance at the magic coming out of the shell.

Something moves inside the photograph, like a face: a trembling mouth, two deep-set eyes, a tear. My mind explodes. Mother!

And it is Mother. Through the shell-projected moving picture, she's talking to me – although I can't hear her and don't know how to make the shell emit sounds. I can't even read my mother's lips, hard as I try.

But when Rose thrusts her plump right hand straight through the projection, trying to catch the face inside, Mother's image fades out.

"What have you done?" I yell.

"I'm so-sorry," Rose says. "I wanted to touch her. Ca-can you bring her back?"

"I don't know." Again I warm up the magic shell, rubbing it with my sweaty palms. To my relief Mother's moving picture shows up once more. I clasp the shell tightly to raise its temperature – I figure the warmer it gets, the clearer the picture I'll get. Maybe this time I'll get sound.

Rose looks ecstatic, while I feel like crying to have my mother with me in this lost underground corner the world.

And then, with a dim voice, my mother speaks to me. She tells me that for the time being she has turned into a falling star, that she brought me here on her tail, that she's watching over me. When she's not gliding through the sky, she floats like a water lily on the fountain of stars by the Aquarius constellation, between Capricorn and Pisces.

Mother says I shouldn't be afraid of this new world I've found at the end of the Magic Corridor. It's my destiny to be here in Rondelia for now. And when I go back to Salem, Mother will return to green sap, like all the herbs witches of the past who live in the Ghostly-Trees Forest.

"But be careful!" Mother says. "No Salem magic can protect you here."

She smiles at me and vanishes into the shell.

Yet Mother leaves me with a tangible proof of her presence: a tear in my left hand. I touch it with the tip of my tongue. It tastes sweet like sugar cane, the way our witch-family tears have always tasted.

I'm happy that although I may be lost, I can still get in touch with my mother.

As I put the shell back in my pack, Rose lies sprawled on my bed, crying and saying that she wants to see her mother.

"Bu-but I don't have a shell!" she manages between sobs.

How can I help her? I remember the little poem Mother taught me the day I lost my hummingbird, the one with orange-and-blue wings and a golden beak.

"Draw it," Mother said. "Every day. Then you won't feel it missing so badly and you'll always have it with you in your drawings."

"Draw your mother," I say, "from your imagination."
Rose's fanged face lights up.
"Draw her eyes and nose, her lips and ears, her hair and
hands,
Draw her like flower, like river, like forest, like sea,
Draw her in the colors of earth, water, fire, and wind,
Draw her in spring, summer, autumn, and winter."

4. The Roma Spell-Casters

Sunday night is like a bottle of black paint.

Red, the Hawks, Zelda, and I pop up the last sewer lid before the western city limit. We're heading for the dreadful orphanage hidden in the woods.

We sneak behind oaks and birches, we crawl through shrubs of bramble, we creep through blueberries and daisies, and surround the orphanage.

With its barred windows and dogs barking on leashes, the sinister building looks like a prison.

I check the sky for Mother. There are no stars above, as if the moon scared them all away.

Black Suits talk in the darkness, drinking from bottles they break on the ground afterward. They're careless of the crickets and caterpillars, fireflies and ladybugs that live in little mansions made of clover and grass. The Black Suits ooze their usual rotten odor, and they swear, coughing from too much smoking. They say that soon they'll "check on the vampire and pluck his fangs out."

"We'd better hurry," Red says. He waves at the V-kids with his left arm, meaning they should close in.

A V-kid imitates a howl – which is the signal that we're taking over the orphanage. Red jumps on the first Black Suit. Fangs gleaming, the V-kids throw their little bodies on their prey. Zelda follows them, biting two Black Suits at a time. She throws her python over petrified Black Suits, then proceeds to knock to the ground everything that happens to interfere with her robust advance: barking dogs, Black Suits, orphanage guards.

"Kids!" she yells upon reaching the orphanage's door, "be ready! We're coming to take you home."

My face covered in ash, my jeans ripped, I throw stones into the enemy with a slingshot.

All goes well until a Black Suit jumps over Red, catches him by the neck, and tries to choke him before Red can bite back. Red's face turns livid, and his tongue sticks out. He's out of breath, and all the V-kids and Zelda and her python are busy finishing off the others. Which leaves me!

But how dare I attack a Black Suit? They almost got me – twice.

When Red's eyes turn upside down, I direct a chubby stone from my slingshot right into the Black Suit's nape. Straight target!

The creature bolts, hisses, and drops Red. Twisting on its heels, it heads toward me, its eyes bulging with rage.

I panic and zigzag among fighting bodies -- my usual rabbit tactic. But the Black Suit is getting ever so close.

"Zelda!" I yell.

Nothing.

"Midgets, Hawks!"

They're digging into the enemy's necks, sucking blood.

I'm back in a circle where the Black Suit held Red hostage. But Red is gone.

I stumble on a pebble and sprawl flat to the ground, just when the Black Suit is behind me. I'm wheezing and the knuckle on my forehead hurts. I crawl, hoping I'll still gain some distance. The stench is already all over me. Soon the creature's hands will be too. I close my eyes.

But nothing happens. How is this possible?

There's a powerful smash, then splashes of mud fall on my face and jeans, soiling Meow. The mud keeps splattering on the ground, melting with a hiss.

"We're even now!" Red says, smirking, his fangs glowing red and black. He pulls me to my feet and offers me a handkerchief. "There, you look better without Black Suit dirt on your nose."

I thank him, humble and tired. How many times does he have to save my life? And did I just save his?

We enter the orphanage. A strong smell of urine hits me. Red says he remembers the unmistakable odor.

The orphans are dressed in rags and lie on beds without sheets, pillows, or blankets. And they smell bad, like they haven't taken a shower in weeks. Some have bad coughs; others moan, saying they've got fever. Others cry for their mothers, fathers, or grandparents.

There's no sign of a doll or a teddy bear – only iron bars: in the dormitories and in the hallways, in the empty kitchen and in the restrooms.

I accompany Zelda, who walks from one bed to another, helping the kids stand up. The V-kids carry them out. When the last child is out and safe, the V-kids tell the orphans about the fabulous Cathedral, where there's plenty of food and toys.

Red and I head for the cellar – where, according to the orphanage director's forced confession, Mr. D is kept prisoner.

We fight with the underground door. When we break it open, we find the great vampire sitting in the dark squalid cellar among cobwebs, rats, and broken lightbulbs. He's quiet and perfectly still, like a statue.

"Mr. D," I whisper. He blinks at me twice, his eyes filled with tears.

He hasn't changed his lizard shape yet. He tries to stand up but can barely move his limbs. A dozen holes pierce Mr. D's body, as if an army of rodents has gnawed him. But what's with his fangs?

Broken!

I stand mute and horrified at the sight of the tortured vampire. There goes my chance of ever reaching Transcarpathia, of ever reuniting with my last living relative.

"These darn Black Suits!" Red says. "Only Zaraza's spells can save him now."

Mr. D lies unconscious on a rug a dozen V-kids carry on their shoulders through the sewers.

We're heading for the Enchanted Forest, at the northern limit of Bookrest. This gives Red some time to tell me that the Roma spell-casters' clan is related to the horse trainers, the tinkers, the painters, the circus, and the musicians' Roma clans.

"They live spread throughout the Enchanted Forest," Red says. "The spells these Romas cast are the strongest. They last from a one-hour toothache to a twenty-four-hour cold, and from a one-month amnesia to a one-year family feud."

By the Salem witches' wands! What a powerful magic. Surely I need to ask the Roma magicians to help me out with a spell that should make me, once and for all, in the eyes of my class the dearest apprentice witch of them all. Will Mrs. Snippety Smith refuse me chocolates any more? No, for her mouth would clasp shut forever and she wouldn't be able to eat. Will Chrysanthemum Crown dare poke fun at me? No, for her red curly hair would fall out and she'd look bald and ugly like a wicked witch.

Out of the sewers, a rotten piece of wood with clunky letters on which the first stars throw a weak light welcomes us:

The Enchanted Forest

Red guides us on the dew-wet grass under a canopy of leaves that barely filters the moonlight. The buzzing of bumblebees, the shrilling of crickets, the hammering of woodpeckers, the warbling of nightingales remind me of the Ghostly-Trees Forest.

"This forest is alive," Red says, brushing against a few birch leaves that rustle, striking their kin on an adjacent bough. The leaves flutter, snapping from one branch to another, from one birch tree to the next, then onto the firs, oaks, and pines nearby, then deep into the forest.

"What did you do to the leaves?" I say.

"I've sent Zaraza a message that we're here," Red says. He explains that the Romas believe leaves are magic messengers, and if you brush up against them, they read your thoughts and send them to whomever you want.

Suddenly the colors around us light up, like they're on fire. The trees come to life, their branches bowing in a salute. We stop and listen to the music coming from the depths of the forest.

In the eerie moonlight, the fluorescent colors flow and decompose in small dots. They mix into new shades, turning from green to red, from blue to orange, from yellow to purple – until the entire forest looks like a painting gallery come to life.

A creature shows up from behind an old oak. But since the colors are still fluid, when the creature approaches, it looks as if it were walking through a wet canvas.

"Zaraza," Waltz whispers.

Zaraza's charcoal-black hair covers her tanned shoulders. Although she resembles Zelda, she looks more human than her sister. For one thing, she doesn't have fangs – she's not a vampire. I'm drawn to her petunia-shaped skirt, on which the colors of autumn play. Sometimes it's orange, then red, then burgundy.

"Welcome," she says in a voice that sounds like rustling leaves. "I've been waiting for you. My sisters told me they met Marigold at the Cathedral."

I greet Zaraza but stand back, intimidated, knowing she can throw strange spells like no witchcraft we use in Salem.

She leads us through the Enchanted Forest, while our clothes get smeared with colored dots, lines, and stripes, until we reach a wall of quivering ivy leaves. Zaraza touches them and they withdraw, fluttering. We pass through the opening, and the plant-wall closes behind us, growing thicker with a few new branches.

We're on the other side, right in the midst of the Roma spell-casters' camp.

Thirteen scarlet bonfires light the glade like little moons.

A dozen wagons gather in a circle, their canopies shredded from sunburn and snow. Their wooden wheels have lost two or three spokes, some even their hubs and rims.

Peacocks wander around, shrilling, their feathers fanned like evening gowns. On their tails a black eye blinks as the birds' plumage flutters.

A noise of metal striking metal comes from behind a wagon. Two boys leap and twist in a rhythmic dance of knives. They clap their hands and heels, and play with the knives in and out of their boots, in and out of their mouths.

A few women with plaited long hair webbed with golden coins smoke pipes. "Little one," they call me with strange sorceresses' voices, "let us show you the future in beans, coffee grounds, and tea leaves."

Others spit in a bowl called Destiny – as Zaraza refers to it. I approach the bowl in awe. Back in Salem we cannot guess our fate or look into the future – it's said only the wicked witches can.

But Zaraza stops me. "You can't look. Destiny will blind you!"

I withdraw just in time. The bowl erupts in a hissing cloud of ash and bubbles.

Halfway through the camp, a girl belly-dances to the notes of a sad song a boy plays on a scarlet violin.

At the other end of the glade, several circus kids jump on trampolines, comb the long hair of a magnificent brown-spotted race horse, play a flute that makes a boa rise out of a wicker basket, and feed fish to a yellow dancing bear.

The V-kids put the rug with a senseless Mr. D in the midst of the glade, surrounded by bonfires. Zaraza dances around the fires, playing with her skirt. All of a sudden, she starts singing an old Roma song. Her voice sounds grave, otherworldly.

"What is this song?" I ask an old woman from the Destiny-bowl group.

"It's the Romas' Magic Song of Life, my child."

"And what do the words mean?"

"They mean that since they left India many centuries ago, the Romas have traveled long roads and have met many a beautiful brother and sister. But they're all dead now." She holds her skirts and braids, and sings the refrain together with Zaraza: "Oh Roma, oh fellow Roma, oh Roma. . ."

The entire camp is one giant voice.

As the depths of the forest resonate with this magic song, turning the colors fluid again, a strange white cloud made of all the Romas' breathes covers Mr. D.

The cloud enters his nostrils. Mr. D changes his shape back to vampire, complete with a black satin cloak and fedora. His body jerks and shakes like a marionette's.

Thunder cracks the sky in two: one side red, the other black. The red side grows into a red cloud that melts into red rain, dripping into Mr. D's now open mouth. He jolts once more and at last wakes up – fresh, his fangs shining in the moonlight, his glare fierce.

I stand there petrified. No witch back home has ever done anything like this.

The sky stretches like a curtain of velvet. All the clouds have gone.

Upon seeing Zaraza, Mr. D blushes and twists his hands, his eyelids fluttering in distress.

By the Salem witches' wands! What's the use of being the greatest vampire in the world if you look like a clumsy teenager when you're in love?

At Mr. D's call, the Romas have now reappeared from their wagons, their hiding posts.

"Tell me," Mr. D asks Zaraza, "what have your maps shown you lately?"

At her sign, the Roma spell-casters knock on the bark of a thick elm. The bark opens up like a book with all sorts of symbols and charts.

"Finally, I got the magic plans," Zaraza says, her skirt turning burgundy.

Forests and seas, dragons and gates, castles and tunnels move on the bark, as if they're alive.

"By my father's Dracula blade!" Mr. D yells, looking at the bark, "Is this what you foretell me?" He throws his fedora on the ground.

"What's the matter, Mr. D?" I ask, surrounded by circus kids.

He keeps silent, his fangs biting his blood-red lower lip.

"Like it or not, this is my prophecy." Zaraza turns her back to the great vampire. Her skirt has turned the color of sunset.

"What prophecy?" I ask, while the Romas glance at the bark in silence.

Zaraza explains that Mr. D wanted to know how to beat the Black Suits. "But nothing is ever clear on my live maps. That's why my predictions keep moving on the bark."

"But what's the meaning of all this?" I ask, pointing at the changing charts.

"It means anything you want, as long as you have a plan!" Zaraza says.

A plan? But of course. "I have a plan!" I say, almost yelling.

The camp stares at me, whispering unknown Roma words. Clouds float again in the sky.

"You do?" Zaraza says, the corners of her eyes slanting upward, like a cat's.

"Yes! We're on our way to Transcarpathia -- isn't that so, Mr. D? We need to get there before the autumn equinox."

Zaraza glares at me, then at Mr. D.

"She's right, you know." Mr. D's voice sounds invigorated, and he drops his fedora back on his bald head.

"Well, in that case," Zaraza says with her grave sorceress's voice – which gives me a shudder, for I imagine she's ready to cast a spell – "here are two Roma spells." In her right hand strange liquids simmer in glass vials. "When you're in danger, use them." She explains that a one-hour paralyzing magic comes out of the green ampoule and a twenty-four-hour terrible witchcraft breaks out of the red vial.

By the Salem witches' wands! I take the little bottles with their boiling potions, which leave me no doubt as to their mighty powers. I wrap them in two chestnut leaves and drop them in my knapsack. Thanks to the Romas I can now use magic before

58

witch age, when apprentices in Salem become witches and are entitled to use wands.

Supposedly only Mrs. Snippety Smith's daughter tried to use spells before her rightful witch time. She was eleven, one year short of graduating from the Pointed-Hats Wizardry School, and didn't know how to handle magic very well. That's when the wicked witches found her and stole her soul. When the tragedy happened, three years ago, mother made me swear I'd never use magic before I reached thirteen.

But in Rondelia I can. And if I can give a helping hand with the Underground, I might even become a hero.

Before Mr. D and Zaraza head into the depths of the forest, Zaraza catches a firefly and drops it in my left hand. Careful not to release it, I let the firefly crawl inside my kaleidoscope. The tube turns into a delicate lantern, beaming a quivering blue light.

When at last fatigue overtakes my gloom, I fall asleep on a patch of warm grass. I dream that the firefly flew all the way back to the Theater of Vaudeville, where it freed all the fireflies held captive in lightbulbs.

At midnight something shakes me – vigorously. Three kids from the circus group chatter around me. I don't open my eyes, pretending I don't hear them. Hopefully they'll let me sleep. But they're on a quest.

"Wake up," Red says. "The kids want to show you a secret – is that right, boys?"

I squint at Red. I squint at the kids. They point at the woods.

"Come on," they say, "before we wake up the camp."

Groggy, I get to my feet and drag behind Red, Waltz, and the circus kids. We pass through glades thick with fireflies and along ponds clogged with water lilies – the site of an ongoing competition of croaking. We tread through a forest of tall ferns, until I lose all sense of direction. But the circus kids walk with confidence.

We reach a dense silent forest. I can't hear the woodpecker, the jay, or the nightingale, the rustling leaves or the breezing wind. Nor can I hear Red or the boys walking. And why can't I hear my own steps on the ground covered with twigs that should be crackling beneath my feet? This really scares me.

When I call Red and nothing comes out of my mouth, the silence around me is deep, like an abyss. Terrified, I leap in Red's direction and catch him by the sleeve. He turns, and I wave my hands around my ears and mouth, signaling that I can't hear a thing.

Red stops the kids, who don't seem surprised. Thumbs up, they signal that everything is okay. Red and I follow them through the silent forest. When we reach a glowing meadow, as I put my feet on the ground the grass suddenly swishes in the wind and my jeans rub softly against my skin. The crickets return, and the autumn's fallen leaves crumble under our feet.

"What was that?" I ask.

"Yeah, what was it?" Red asks.

"These are the Mute Woods," a kid says. "We knew they existed somewhere around here, but we only discovered them last week. We didn't tell anybody." He explains that when they first got into the woods, they pressed their ears against oaks and pines and to the leaf-covered ground. "For a whole day we tried to make a sound, but we couldn't make one or hear one." That's when they came up with a theory: there may be a void underneath the woods that sucks all the sounds into its depths.

"I never thought Rondelia had such strange, powerful woods," Red says, his face lit with wonder.

"Neither did we," the kid says. "We'll use these woods to capture Black Suits – "

"Great idea!" Red says, then turns toward me. "Marigold, why don't you tell the boys about your Magic Corridor?"

"First, it's not mine," I say, blushing, not sure they won't mock me. "But it's true. I came to this country through a Magic Corridor. It took me through the Milky Way galaxy."

Red winks at the boys. "Told you, it's the same corridor the Black Suit used to get to the last herbs witch of Salem – "

"No way!" the kids say.

"Yep! And this is her daughter, Marigold," Red says.

"A witch?" the kid who says this sounds panicky.

"Not yet," I say, "but in three years . . ."

"I'll pass a test and become a powerful witch." Red imitates me with a high-pitched voice.

The kids laugh.

I blush. One day I'll show this funny jester Red why it's never a good idea to mess with a Salem witch!

We stare at the moon, listen to the humming of the meadow, then head back through the Mute Woods.

The silence in there is so deep that I try to focus on the inner sounds of my body, even wonder if I might hear my thoughts. But I can't hear anything, not my heart, or the rubbing of my lips, or my sneeze when I sniff a pine cone.

Red runs and yells, laughing at us, hopping like a clown. Maybe he thinks it's fun that no matter what he does, nobody can hear him. He climbs trees and glides down their trunks, throws rocks in a small pond, and imitates animals and birds – though nobody can tell which ones, since we can't hear him roaring, barking, chirping.

We walk out of the forest, and sound returns. The kids make Red and me swear we'll never tell anybody about the Mute Woods.

"Silence over silence over silence!" the five of us pledge, stabbing the tip of our index fingers with a pin.

Solemnly we watch our fingers release droplets of blood, which we let trickle onto the porous surface of a leaf that turns red. We swear again, imagining that the leaf has somehow become sacred through our oaths and blood.

Just when we've buried the leaf between two juniper shrubs, desperate hollers reach us from the camp. Gunshots resonate throughout the forest.

The Romas flee into the woods.

"Black Suits!" the circus kids yell. "They must've entered the forest." With that they're gone, back in the direction of the Mute Woods.

"Silence over silence over silence," Red says, winking at me. "Got to go now. I promised the kids I'd help them catch Black Suits in those silent places."

He shows me a giant lizard – Mr. D – approaching us through the glade. He throws me that unmistakable blue gaze, then says, "And let me know if you ever find your relative in Transcarpathia."

"But Red. . ." I try to catch his sleeve. "Stay, please!"

"Bye-bye, Marigold of Salemmm . . . " he says, and without hesitation vanishes after the circus kids.

Boys!

"Will the Romas be all right?" I ask Mr. D, hopping onto his back.

"Don't worry. Zaraza's magic will save them." Mr. D explains that Roma magic has killed far more Black Suits than have vampire bites. In any case, he's still weak from the Black Suits' latest experiments on his fangs and isn't up for another fight. But he is up for a gallop to Transcarpathia.

By the Salem witches' wands! It's about time.

The Enchanted Forests comes to life again. Its colors grow fluid, staining the Black Suits, blinding them, clogging their clothes, making them fall, sticking them to the ground. The forest pours rains of guache, oil, and aquarelle on the Black Suits' bayonets, hatchets, and axes. Leaves drop like stones on their heads, branches smash their faces, stumps catch them by the legs and drag them into the depths of the forest.

5. Escape to the City of Whispers

$\mathcal{W}$e're speeding a hundred miles an hour throughout the Enchanted Forest. But no matter how fast we go, the Black Suits are on our tracks: they run-glide, mollusk style. Shooting and yelling, they scare the critters that take refuge into tree nests and earth holes.

Since Mr. D can hardly keep up the fast pace, we take a shortcut through a meadow covered with daisies and surrounded by statuesque evergreens.

A golden gate rises in the midst of the meadow. Above it, a plate reads:

THE LAWS OF TIME

By the Salem witches' wands! What is this?

Mr. D sees wonder in my eyes. "A Time Gate!" he says.

"You mean, a gate through time?"

I look back to check for Black Suits. Their hollers get closer.

Breathless, Mr. D points at the gate. "Should we?"

"What? Go through it?"

"I don't see another way out," Mr. D says, exhaling steam.

He thrusts his right foot forward in a big stride, then vanishes: his muzzle, his claws, his iron scales, his lizard tail. He yells from the invisible other side, like he's fallen into a hollow well.

Is he all right? But I don't have time to hesitate, because right now a Black Suit jumps at me from behind a pine tree. The creature is ready to snatch my backpack -- or is it heading for my neck? Its stinky, dark, muddy hands are barely a foot away.

Whatever might be on the other side of the gate is better than what's on this one – unless it's the Land of Endless-Night. Impossible! That's only a Salem story.

I put my right foot through the gate. A strong force sucks at my entire body, as if a giant vacuum cleaner is swallowing me up.

I'm falling, traveling again through a tunnel, packed in a bubble of air. Occasionally giant thunders spike in the darkness around. On a closer look, they resemble sequences of film running on wheels that count years like seconds.

In the first footage, people gather in streets, chanting under a tricolor flag that reads: "*Liberté, égalité, fraternité, ou la mort!* Paris, 1789."

Their gunshots follow me into a London image, where a severed head is stuck on a pole above Westminster Hall. The year is 1661, and a banner under the head reads: "Cromwell."

In a 1350 projection, Europeans crawl on streets chased by a black hooded creature that threateningly waves a scythe and looks like a Black Suit. "The Black Death!" someone yells before falling, covered in plague boils.

In China, a man shows me how to make paper out of bamboo fiber. And a poet who signs his letters "Ovidius Naso" dedicates an elegy to Rome and dies upon reaching a black sea, just when this vortex flings me flat to the ground.

I squish Meow, who scurries on the back of my T-shirt. Although my jeans have tears everywhere, I'm proud of them – they're living proof of my courage.

To my relief Mr. D stands right in front of me, all dressed up in his elegant cloak and with his fedora completing his image.

"What year is it?" I ask.

"1938," Mr. D says, glancing at his watch.

"How come you can stand the sunlight? "

"No problem, kid. This is a sun from the past. It can't hurt me. It's not like it's real."

The strangeness of our situation strikes me hard. Rushing to escape the Black Suits, I completely forgot.

"But Mr. D," I say, "how will we go back?"

Mr. D's brows draw together. "We'll just. . .have to find another Time Gate."

He explains that traveling in time is a great science, that we can go back in time, and from the past, forward into the future, which is our present time. But we can't go beyond our present into another future. "That's something only time travelers can do, and only in exceptional cases."

Have I just traveled a Magic Corridor through time? By the Salem witches' wands! There are not one but two kinds of Magic Corridors: one to travel through space, another through time.

Women wearing white lace gloves and large-brimmed hats and men in elegant suits hurry around us. Although we walk right in their midst, not one of them so much as glances at us.

"Can't they see us?" I ask Mr. D.

"That's the trick when you go back in time – you become invisible, so you can't interfere with history."

Funny. It's like when I walked through the Mute Woods with Red and the circus kids, and we yelled to the moon and back, and nobody could hear us.

"And where is the other Time Gate?" I ask impatient to resume our voyage to Transcarpathia.

"Haven't got a clue, but I know someone here who has –" Mr. D says relaxed.

Now I am panicky.

"This is old Bookrest," he says relaxed, pointing around like a tourist guide. He explains that the Roma magicians believe cities never die. They're recreated from the thoughts and memories of their one-time inhabitants. "This is living proof that the Bookrest of the thirties never disappeared."

We pass between two classic colonnades and enter the bright foyer of a concert hall. A senior couple emerges from the second floor. They take the spiraling white marble staircase down and wave at Mr. D.

"The Steins, my friends." Mr. D opens his arms in a large welcoming gesture. He says that over the years the Steins have helped him out with all sorts of things, from getting medicines to finding rare books and piano scores. "They're time travelers."

Time travelers?

"They go back and forth in time and help people fight for justice." Mr. D says the Steins have several time residences.

By the Salem witches' wands!

"One is in the Bookrest of the thirties, another residence is in the Paris of the nineties." Mr. D says the Steins lived for centuries in Prague, where they come from originally. Last time he saw them, they were just returning from Leonardo da Vinci's Florence. They had nurtured Leonardo back to life after one of his experiments with flying machines went bad. "Anyway, they know where the other Time Gate is."

The time travelers are standing in front of us.

"Who's the little girl?" the fair-skinned woman asks, peering at me with green eyes.

"She is Marigold, my protégé," Mr. D says.

Since when am I Dracula's protégé? Maybe Red told him how I fought at the orphanage, maybe Waltz whispered to him how I helped the Midgets at the Cathedral?

I nod to both Steins. But a little thought keeps bugging me: If they're time travelers, are they also invisible to the people around us?

I still haven't uttered a word. But Meow is more daring and sniffs Mrs. Stein, probably because of her sweet lilac perfume.

"Hurry!" the Steins say as we leave the concert hall. They explain that they're in a rush off to fifteenth-century Germany to help Johannes Gutenberg develop his printing machine. That's why they can't join Mr. D's fight against the Black Suits, and that's why they'd like to give Mr. D something special – "for the Underground." So before they take us to the Time Gate, they say we have to go to the City of Whispers.

Great! It's already Monday noon. Can't they see I'm in a hurry?

"Excuse me, ma'am," I ask Mrs. Stein, "what is the City of Whispers?"

"My dear, the City of Whispers is the ancient district of Old Bookrest." She explains that only ghosts live there. But because they don't have real voices, the ghosts whisper, "hence the name City of Whispers."

"Are these ghosts wicked?" I ask.

"It's not like they're good or bad, they're just ghosts of past wars." Mrs. Stein tells me that some ghosts were victors, others defeated. But since they died together in the same battles, they live together ever afterward, sharing the same fate.

It strikes me that the streets around me bear no names. I approach a sign, and the letters fade out, leaving it gray. I head for a signpost, and the same thing happens.

"Why?" I ask Mrs. Stein, pointing.

"Because in your present, in the nineties, the streets will have changed anyway. They just don't want you to see their past names."

By the time we pass a street, the houses' façades have changed, the gravel road has turned to pavement, and new faces of people and new models of cars are rushing around us.

In fact, the entire network of streets shifts like a live maze: Palazzos disappear and piazzas burst in their places, parks vanish and boutiques replace them instead.

"But how will we be able to go back?" I ask.

"Don't worry," Mr. Stein says, "we know Bookrest's street map by heart, a hundred years from now."

We reach a gate that opens to a mysterious dark-green pond. On it, a tarnished plate reads:

CITY OF WHISPERS

A green willow rustles leaves on the quiet surface. It strikes me that everything around this pond is green: the leaves, the nightingales, the insects, the translucent reflection of this past sky.

"What tree is this?" I ask Mrs. Stein, who seems to know everything around here.

"It's an Oracle," Mrs. Stein says. "Listen!"

A voice coming from the leaves says, "Run, run, run. Death is coming. You will all die. Run, run, run. . ."

Wait a minute. If this is 1938, the Oracle must be predicting the Second World War. And I'm in Europe, right where the war is going to start, right when death will come and kill many of the people I've just seen in the streets!

"Excuse me," I say, frantic, "are we going to be here long?"

"Just until we find the Golem," Mrs. Stein says calmly.

The Golem? What or who is this?

I glance at Mr. D.

"Not a vampire," Mr. D says. He bows and whispers into my ear, "Don't worry, Marigold, I promised I'd help you find your relative, and so I shall. Cross my heart and hope to undie!"

Ghosts of children, women, and men emerge from walls, roofs, and pavement. They float around – and through! – me. Eyes half-closed, the corners of their mouths turned down, they look sad and bereft. Yet they are not interested in us, and drift away to gather around the Oracle-willow.

"Are these the ghosts of the past wars?" I ask Mrs. Stein, whispering.

"Yes, dear. They always circle the Oracle-willow in the evening to listen to its words and try to remember who they are." She tells me that since the ghosts can never recall their names – otherwise, they'd return from the dead – they keep coming every day, hoping the willow will awaken them. But nobody from this time except the ghosts believes this Oracle's predictions about the future.

"Why?" I ask.

"Because life's too beautiful to be lived, and nobody from the present ever worries about the future. If they did, their lives would be sad, and living wouldn't be worthwhile."

The ghosts swarm around the willow, swooshing in the air, dropping on its branches, skittering on the lake like they're skating.

Who said ghosts are scary?

Suddenly I'm being lifted into the air. Two ghosts hold me under my armpits.

"Help!" I yell at Mr. D and the Steins, who are busy looking at an old map of Bookrest and don't seem to notice.

The ghosts carry me over my companions' heads. At the last second, Mr. D's long hand reaches my shoes but fails to hold onto them. I'm afraid I'll fall in the green pond and drown like a fly in a bottle of ink.

As the Steins grow smaller, at last the ghosts drop me on the willow's topmost branch. I yell for Mr. D.

"Hey, what are you doing with the girl?" he hollers at the ghosts.

"You're trespassing time. You're not supposed to be here," the Oracle-willow says with a swishing voice.

"But dear," Mrs. Stein says, "we're time travelers. The girl and this tall gentleman are our guests." She points at me shivering on the top green branch and at a furious Mr. D, his lower lip trembling under his fangs.

"Nevertheless, they're trespassers, and I'm taking this girl," the willow says. "She's a prisoner of time."

In vain Mrs. Stein tries to convince the willow that we're not going to harm history or change its course, time, or events. The Oracle stands firm in its decision to keep me its prisoner forever.

The ghosts begin to play with my hair and hop on my branch, and in general try to do everything to make me fall into the pond.

I cry, "Somebody, please, do something!"

"All right," the willow says. "I'm afraid something very bad is about to happen. But my readings of the future have been blurry lately. If one of you can tell me three important historical events that'll happen in the next few years, I promise to release the girl."

"But we can't possibly do that," the Steins say in one voice. "You know the Laws of Time forbid it."

"Do you want the girl back or not?" the Oracle-willow says.

In the midst of the squabble I get an idea. "How about we cover our ears so we won't be able to hear anything?" I yell at Mrs. Stein.

"What, dear?"

"She's right," Mr. D says. "Marigold and I will cover our ears, and when you tell the willow what will happen in the future, we won't hear you, and you won't have broken the Laws of Time. Unless – "

"What, dear?"

"Unless the ghosts hear you," Mr. D says.

"Oh, no, dear," Mrs. Stein says, waving her hand, "they're ghosts of past wars. Nothing from the future can affect them. All they want to know is their past and who they are."

"Are you ready for the bargain?" the willow asks.

"Ready, dear," Mrs. Stein says, while Mr. D and I cover our ears so tightly we couldn't hear fireworks going off. I even close my eyes, pretending I'm not ten feet up, hanging from an jade-green willow that's talking to a time traveler across a lake, in a time past.

The willow jerks to its roots – three times. I figure it must be from the shock of learning what's going to happen. It starts to sob so violently that it loses dozens of leaves, and scares off the ghosts. I fear that in the end I'll have to plunge into the pond and swim for my life.

But the willow stretches and bends like a chute. I slide to the ground.

"Run, run, run. . ." the Oracle-willow calls after me with its scary voice.

No sooner have I reached the Steins and Mr. D than the Oracle-willow spreads all of its branches on the pond's surface. Like mouths, the branches sip the water down to the pond's bottom while the willow grows fat. The entire pond is now in its trunk.

Hidden in the mud of the pond's green bottom, an object shines in the moonlight.

"Take it," the Oracle-willow says. "It's the Golem."

The willow tells us its readings of the future foretold that we'd come here searching for the Golem.

The Steins' eyes loom. They hurry down the newly-born ravine leading to the bottom of the desiccated pond. They dig and dig until they remove a glittering object that looks like a jar the size of a censer. This Golem must be pretty small.

Wheezing, the Steins climb out of the ravine.

"The Golem of Prague," Mr. Stein says, pointing to the jar.

Mrs. Stein takes a handkerchief from her purse to wipe off a few tears.

Finally, I dare ask, "Pardon me, who is the Golem?"

"The Golem was a giant," Mr. Stein says, "a hero made of clay who protected the Jewish people living in sixteenth-century Prague." He explains he'd just married Mrs. Stein and was living in the ghetto of Prague when – using Kabbala chants – Rabbi Loew made the Golem with clay from the Moldavka River's bank.

"The Golem had no mind of its own, but it had mighty powers," Mrs. Stein says. "It fearlessly defended the ghetto." She tells us that when the creature was eventually returned to clay, the rabbi left its remains in the attic of Prague's great temple.

Later, when a fire burned down the Jewish ghetto, many people snuck in the temple and took a handful of clay, hoping its magic would save them from future dangers.

Still, the bulk of the Golem clay burned and its ash rose to the sky, where it condensed into a star the size of the Golem. But to this day nobody knows where this star is, and nobody has ever seen the Golem again.

Mr. Stein lifts the jar in the moonlight. "We also took some Golem clay dust."

"Are you done?" the Oracle-willow asks. "Hurry, I see it in my readings, the Black Suits are on your tracks!"

"Black Suits?" the four of us say, frantic.

The willow nervously spits all the water back in the pond, then yells, "Why did I ever believe you? You said you wouldn't change history! But now it's too late. Run, run, run – "

"But they weren't supposed to travel here?" Mr. Stein says. "The Laws of Time forbid it.– "

"Maybe they're getting stronger," Mrs. Stein says, wiping a few more tears. She's heard rumors that the Black Suits have started to travel through the Magic Corridors.

I want to tell her about the Black Suit who traveled to Salem and killed my mother, and the ones that chased us throughout the Enchanted Forest before we crossed the Time Gate. But the Oracle-willow hollers like mad, "Watch out! Black Suits. Over there!"

A pack of Black Suits shows up from the other side of the pond and jumps on Mr. D. Again the vampire has turned into a lizard covered with iron scales. He plunges his fangs into the Black Suits' necks. Others, he chokes with his bare hands. Yet the Black Suits are strong. They reach for knives under their trenchcoats and thrust to stab Mr. D in the chest, back, and arms. Mr. D hits them with his lizard tail. The Black Suits pull out hatchets. But Mr. D is quick again and smashes them to the ground.

How much longer can he resist?

The Steins and I withdraw behind the willow. Desperate, we try to climb the tree. But it scatters us back to the ground, and says, "No, you've cheated me. What are these thugs doing here? They're not from this time."

"Please, Oracle-willow, please help us," I say. I explain that I need to go back to the 90's and find my last living parent before the autumn equinox, in just six days; that I am an orphan but also a witch apprentice from Salem.

"A Salem witch?" the willow says. "Well, in that case. . ."

It sends its branches into the ground around the pond. A ten-foot-high wall of green thorny vines grows, separating us from the Black Suits who keep fighting and dying under Mr. D's fangs.

A thorny stem hisses at me. The vines are alive!

Meow sniffs the plants. Terrified, she climbs on my chest, trying to tear off the hem of my T-shirt, probably trying to walk out of it.

"Hurry, let's sing the spells!" Mrs. Stein says.

Mr. Stein wipes off the jar with his sleeve and murmurs some incantations.

Spells from the Kabbala?

But nothing happens. The Golem doesn't show up. Mrs. Stein sings a sad melody, but with no result other than mellowing the willow.

I get an idea. I search through my backpack, take out Mother's magic shell, and close my eyes.

"What have you got there, dear?" Mrs. Stein asks.

I explain that the shell can connect me to my mother, who is a falling star in the fountain of the Aquarius constellation.

The Steins look at me skeptically.

Once the shell, warms up, it throws a dim projection in the air: Mother's face.

"Mother, do you know where the Golem star is?" I ask.

She whispers something that to my despair dissolves in the air.

I don't give up. I warm up the shell with more energy, and even the Steins offer to help. The three of us hold the shell until I finally hear Mother saying, "The Golem star is five stars away from me, to the north, in the Heroes' Black Hole. . . ."

The Steins look bewildered.

"What kind of magic is this, dear?" Mrs. Stein asks.

"It's Salem witchcraft," I say. Then I ask Mother, "How can we get in touch with the Golem star?"

"I'll light it up for you, then it's up to you, darling." With that she vanishes back inside the shell.

A shooting star from the Aquarius constellation slashes through clouds and beams light in the darkest spot in the sky. There, a little star we've never seen before begins to twinkle.

The Golem star.

"But how are we going to get to the Golem?" I ask Mrs. Stein.

In silence, she opens the jar, takes a bit of clay dust, and spreads it on the ground.

The willow yells, dangling its branches in the air. But the Golem star grows bigger and shinier, like it's approaching us.

Mr. Stein powders the ground with a wisp of clay dust, and even I take some and sprinkle it around. And each time we touch and spread the magical dust, the star advances toward us like a comet, until it falls in front of us, making the willow quiver in panic.

The Steins and I hold our breath, astonished at the sight of the ten-foot-tall creature covered in stardust.

By the Salem witches' wands!

The giant gets to his chubby feet. Instead of skin he has a brown layer of solid clay, and he's peering at us with small dark friendly eyes. He has no nose, mouth, or ears on his square head, although a star shines on his forehead. His ripped brown suit has patches on the elbows, knees, and shoulders.

The Golem bows in front of the Steins, blinks, and assumes the position of a soldier – erect, head up, chin pointing forward.

"Can he talk?" I ask.

"No, dear," Mrs. Stein says. "He's mute, but he understands our orders."

Desperate cries resonate from behind the vines.

Mr. D! The Black Suits!

Mr. D is still fighting the last two Black Suits – the others have melted into puddles of mud. He's no longer a lizard but has resumed his vampire shape. His fedora lies dusted on the ground, his cloak slashed by the vines' spines.

As if the Black Suits were not enough, Mr. D bites a live stalk by mistake, and the plant strikes him with its thorns.

Mrs. Stein nods at the Golem.

Barefoot, heavy, and sturdy, the giant takes a large stride toward the site where Mr. D is barely holding off his two attackers. The Golem crushes the furious branches under his huge clay feet and smashes the Black Suits with his thick fingers.

The vine turns black. Like a cornered octopus, it sends all of its tentacles toward the Golem, only to have them torn apart again. The plant hisses, then takes refuge in the ground.

Free at last, Mr. D brushes at his tattered trousers, his face scratched from the thorns, his cloak sliced like a tassel. He thanks the Golem and tries to put on a serious face.

"Who is this fellow?" he asks the Steins.

"The Golem of Prague," Mrs. Stein says.

The Steins explain to an amazed Mr. D all about the Golem and how I helped them bring him from the Heroes' Black Hole.

Mr. D says he recalls a four-century-old book from his Castle Bran's library that told the story of a giant made of clay with unheard-of courage who lived seven forests, seven mountains, and seven rivers away.

"Maybe it was the Golem," he says, glancing with respect at the giant, who occasionally blinks, which seems to be a sign that he understands our words.

The Oracle-willow has turned to a sad shade of dark green.

I say goodbye, but all it says is, "Run, run, run."

"Hurry, now," Mr. Stein says. "Other Black Suits might show up."

We walk out of the City of Whispers. The streets have changed their lights and shops, their homes and cars, the people's ages and fashions. By the time darkness falls over Bookrest and the gaslights illuminate the city like an old black-and-white photograph, we finally reach a silver Time Gate.

"Now, dear," Mrs. Stein says, staring at me, "since we're not coming with you into your present, we'll teach you how to master the Golem." She orders the giant to bend. "The only thing you have to do is touch his star."

"Like this?" Mr. D asks, ready to touch the giant's forehead.

"Stop!" Mr. Stein yells. "You can't do this. You're a vampire."

Mr. D freezes.

"Only time travelers and children with innocent hearts can master the Golem," Mrs. Stein says, glaring at Mr. D.

I smirk. Obviously, I'm the only child around.

"Marigold," Mrs. Stein says, "with your magic shell, you've convinced us that you're a powerful witch – a good witch. You -- "

"Frankly, I'm not even interested in this," Mr. D says. "I have too much to worry about on my own. Taking care of the V-kids, of the entire Underground. . ."

I hope he's not hurt. I peek at him, and he's quick enough to see the glint in my eyes. He winks back at me, waving his hand with its sharp nails, as if saying, "No problem, kid!"

Mrs. Stein places my right hand on the Golem's forehead and says, "There! Now you'll be able to give him orders."

When I remove my hand, something tickles my palm: my jade-green witch line. Now I'll show Red who's the smartest one – and I won't even have to pass the Witchcraft Test.

The Steins wish us good luck and vanish around a corner that changes into a botanical garden. I'm left alone with Dracula and the Golem.

We're ready to enter the Time Gate. Mr. D says we should let the Golem go first. That I should ask him to wait for us on the other side, in our present time.

"Sure," I say, and order the Golem to walk through the gate. After his heavy silhouette disappears, it's my turn.

Off I go in the bubble of air and through the time tornado. Below me, Mr. D is seized in a similar sphere. He looks tired and morose.

I try to cheer him up by showing him a thunder projecting the signing of the Declaration of Independence by the Thirteen Colonies, on July 4, 1776.

As Mr. D watches the Congress representatives taking oaths, I get frantic: Mother's magic shell. By the Salem witches' wands! I left it by the Oracle-willow.

I kick the bubble with my hands and shoes, desperately trying to pierce it with my nails. After repeated attempts, the sphere explodes.

I fall on top of Mr. D's bubble. The collision is so strong, his sphere pops and we both fall, smashing to the ground.

Dizzy, I squint at Mr. D, who's lying on his back. I'm afraid I've killed him – maybe not, he's the undead.

"Are you all right?" I ask him.

"I've been better," he says, his face covered with grit. He peers around, then yells, "We're lost!"

"What?"

"We are lost!"

"You mean we're not back in 1938?"

"You interrupted the time voyage, and we've fallen into who-knows-what year." He says that if time travelers don't finish their voyage, time can catapult them into any year at random – where they have to face any possible historical consequences.

Mr. D is right. I don't recognize anything I saw in 1938. What have I done? Not only are we in a different time, but without the Steins how can we find our way in a city whose street map has changed for good? I'll never be able to find the City of Whispers and Mother's magic shell. And without the magic shell, I'll never be able to reach Mother again.

A tear forces its way down my dusty cheek, then another one. Exhausted, I'm weeping like I haven't wept since Mother died.

Mr. D keeps silent, his cloak tattered, his face scratched and swollen.

"Can we try the Time Gate again?" I ask him.

Before he can answer me, tanks show up from around the corner, ready to blow a shell at us. When the first one comes close enough for me to read Black Suits Army on its side, I freak out.

Mr. D slaps his forehead, looks at his watch, and cries, "Oh, no – we're in 1951, the year when the Black Suits take over Rondelia."

I'm paralyzed.

"Leave!" Mr. D yells at me. "I'll stay here – "

"No, Mr. D!"

"Marigold, the Black Suits will follow you through the Time Gate. And I can't let that happen."

Gently he grabs me from under my armpits and drops me through the Time Gate.

I'm closed in a bubble of air, rushing fast-forward into the future.

Oh, Mr. D! He's left stranded in time and alone, prey to the Black Suits. How am I going to get back together with him? And how am I ever going to reach Transcarpathia?

6. "The Spy"

Back to Bookrest, only five days short of the last autumn equinox of the twentieth century, the Golem and I are walking in silence in the soggy sewer tunnels.

We've barely entered the Cathedral when Red and Waltz run toward me. "Where is Mr. D?" they ask.

"And who's this giant?" Waltz barks.

"Is he with you, or should I call the Hawks?" Red asks, his fangs ready to attack.

"This is the Golem of Prague," I say. "He's my friend." I look into Red's eyes to see what impression my new companion has made on him.

"Really?" Red checks the giant's clay hands while Waltz sniffs at his bare feet.

"As for Mr. D. . ." I gulp and order the Golem to sit near the Vampire Organ.

"What about Mr. D?" Red asks.

"I lost him," I say in a very small voice. I tell them about the Black Suits' ambush and losing Mother's magic shell by the

Oracle-willow, about poking at my bubble of air and falling astray with Mr. D in the Time Corridor.

I close my eyes. What kind of witch are you? I can just hear Red say, dismissing me with his cocky blue gaze. At least he doesn't know that back in Salem they call me "nerd witch."

But to my amazement, Red says, "Perhaps not all is lost."

"Excuse me?" I say, searching through the pack for my "I ? Salem" T-shirt.

He explains that a few years ago, Zelda told him there are many time gates around the world. "And one such gate opens right in the waters of the Sapphire Sea."

A time gate in the middle of a sea? By the Salem witches' wands! Does this mean I still have a chance to get to Transcarpathia?

"But we should leave right away," Waltz says. "Who knows what terrible things might happen to Mr. D if we don't hurry."

Pikes, cuffs, scissors, sunlight, even Black Suits keep circling in my head.

"We caught a spy!" Red says, interrupting my guilty nightmare.

"A spy?"

"Yes, we caught a woman so scary, we've never seen one of her kind before – ever."

"She says she got here by mistake," Waltz says. "But we think she's a spy – a Black-Suits spy."

"Where is she now?" I ask.

First they had to close her in a cave on the western wall of the Cathedral, Red and Waltz say. But she scared the kids so badly that they had to put her in a cage. "She was so mean, she said she'd eat us all," Red says.

"But where did you catch her?" I ask.

"It was the night when the Black Suits attacked the Romas in the Enchanted Forest," Red says. He explains that when he and the circus kids reached the Mute Woods and saw her roaming among trees, they thought she was a Black-Suits spy. She was dressed in a black ragged cotton dress, and her gray short hair stretched in all directions, like a wild boar's. "The minute she saw me and the kids, her eyes glittered like she was mad. She chased us out of the silent forests and threatened to take our souls. That's when I showed her my fangs and she dropped to the ground, yelling this was the Land of Endless-Night."

"The Land of Endless-Night?" My knees are shaking.

Red notices. A few V-kids gather around, their fangs gleaming.

I explain to the vampire children that in the land of witches where I come from, there's an old story about the Land of Endless-Night that existed before Salem was built. "When the native Indians came with the forest and its spirits, they defeated evil Queen Nocturna of the Land of Endless-Night. They settled down in the woods and for the first time allowed the sun to enter the forests." Later, I tell them, when the first witches came and built the town with their magic, the native Indians and Salem witches fought Queen Nocturna, but she refused to leave. Sometimes she would take over the hearts and minds of the newly born and turn them into wicked witches. "But both my mother and I are herbs witches. We're good witches."

"How do you know?" Red asks. His eyes glint strangely.

"Because I have a sign."

"What sign?" Waltz asks.

"I have a four-leafed green clover on my left shoulder blade. I was born with it, and so was Mother. It's our herbs witches' guild sign." I turn my back and push my Meow T-shirt off my left shoulder, showing my birthmark.

The V-kids sniff at my clover sign. Are they going to bite me?

I hurry to cover my shoulder and keep them busy with my story. I tell them that in Salem everybody belongs to a guild. After the great Ash River wars, when the good witches banned the wicked witches from ever entering Salem again, these evil sorcerers took refuge at the Black Hollow Lake.

"Since then, the witches of Salem are divided into five witchcraft guilds. The Herbs' Guild, the one mother and I belong to, is the oldest of all". The herbs witches possess the knowledge of plants, remedies, and poisons. Their sign is the green clover with four leaves. "When I become a real witch three years from now, I'll attend the sacred gatherings dressed only in green, the color of leaves, grass, and caterpillars. And when I die, I'll become green sap frothing in the trunks of trees, gurgling in roots, spurting with life in petals opened overnight. I'll become forest. The Black-Cats' Guild comes next."

"Black-cats witches?" Waltz asks, barking.

"Yes, these witches teach cats to speak and act as assistants in witchcraft." The guild's sign is a black cat sitting, her tail raised like a question mark. It's said that upon their deaths, the souls of the black-cats witches enter into newborn kittens, turning them into new generations of black-cats assistants. And every Tuesday, when we get together in the Ghostly-Trees Forest to celebrate Salem Day – our sacred day of rest – the black-cats witches dress in black and sing surrounded by purring cats.

The V-kids look at me, entranced.

I tell them that the witches belonging to the Brooms' Guild carve brooms out of oak, birch, and chestnut. That they teach them to fly and last through thunder and battle, storm and snow. Their sign is a flying broom and they always dress in scarlet during our Tuesday assemblies. And when they die, they become tree trunks whose wood witches use when they make new loyal flying brooms.

"But the bravest of all are the witches of the Warriors' Guild," I say. They guard Salem against the wicked witches and Queen Nocturna, who come out at times from the Land of Endless-Night. The guild's mark is the spear, and they dress in silver like thunder and fish scales. Upon their deaths, they become thick mist covering Salem overnight – every night – guarding the town against all that is evil. "Last comes the Professors' Guild."

"You've got professors, too?" Red asks.

"They teach us witchcraft and poetry, the history of Salem and its wars." Our professors' sign is the white plume. They carry a feather quill, ready to jot down ideas and poems on a flying companion notebook. "Truth is, I like poetry so much I'd trade my Herbs' Guild position for the Professors'. But since this is impossible in Salem, I've decided that when I become a herbs witch, I'll write all my herbs recipes in verse." I tell them that at our Tuesday congregations, the Professors' Guild dresses in white robes and takes notes on what's been decided regarding Magic and Administration for the coming week.

"But I don't know who belongs to what guild," I say. "I'll find this out only when I turn thirteen, pass the witch test, and become a herbs witch. Until then I'm just a witch apprentice." I smile, hoping my story about Salem has made it clear that I'm only a little girl, not a witch – yet.

Red orders the V-kids to bring in the spy.

The Midgets head for the western wall, while the Hawks spread out, swarming like ants, rushing under their beds, pulling out strange gear. They dress up in golden plates carved with Dracula's dragon symbol, and cover their heads with little shining helmets. Yelling and poised for fight, they begin a military exercise with spears and bats.

"What's with these outfits, and who made them?" I ask Red, who looks cocky in his military gear and directs the Hawks like a general.

"They're for the grand battle, when we'll knock out all the Black Suits from Rondelia," Red says, knocking into his helmet with pride. He explains that the Roma tinkers handcrafted the metal from several alloys. Then the Roma spell-casters threw protective charms on them. "They're impenetrable."

By the Salem witches wands! These V-kids are a true army.

From the back of the grotto, an ugly yet surprisingly familiar voice yells, "I'll pour hot chocolate on you and kill you all. I'll freeze your corpses and sell you as chocolate statues for Halloween!"

The V-kids drag an iron cage in the midst of the Cathedral. They're hanging by its bars like monkeys. They laugh, poking the creature inside the cage, reaching in to pull its skirt and hair, throwing crumbs of bread on its head.

The prisoner inside the cage is none other than my old foe – Mrs. Snippety Smith, fuming with rage. By the Salem witches' wands! What's she doing here?

I close my eyes to block out the ugly vision. But when I open them, Red is in the midst of the noisy bunch.

"So, what do you think of our spy?" he asks me.

"Maaa-rigold!" Mrs. Snippety Smith yells, staring at me, her eyes red with fury.

"Do you know this spy?" Red asks.

The strangeness of the situation doesn't escape me. Although I'd love to take revenge on Mrs. Snippety Smith for all the chocolate she refused me – pretending that I don't know her, that I've never seen her in my life, that she must be an old crazy woman or a wicked witch or even a Black Suit spy – I sigh and say, "She's a witch from Salem, like me. But I don't know what guild she's from."

Silence falls on the V-kids. Red's eyelids have developed a tic. "What?"

"I know her," I say. "She's Mrs. Snippety Smith, from the Magic Cookies Chocolaterie."

"And you swear she's not a spy?" Red asks.

"I don't think so, although I don't understand how she got here."

Could Mayor Icelandia de Winter have given Mrs. Snippety Smith a ticket to the Magic Corridor from Salem to Bookrest? But why?

"Maaa-rigold!" Mrs. Snippety Smith yells again. "Marigold, will you tell these little barbarians to take me out of the cage right this – "

"No way!" a V-kid says, grimacing at her. "She says she'll turn us into chocolates and eat us all, starting with the Midgets."

"And will you?" I ask Mrs. Snippety Smith, a nasty smirk on my face.

"Your mother should've taught you some better manners, Marigold, but now it's too late," Mrs. Snippety Smith says, her face blotchy. "Of course, I won't eat them. I won't eat anyone."

Here I am, my chocolate enemy in front of me, bargaining for release with the V-kids. I tell them she's just a tired Salem witch, partly mad from losing her daughter to the wicked witches of the Black Hollow Lake.

But the V-kids want to keep her locked forever in the cage. I tell them that if they release her, she'll cook them the best chocolates.

"Isn't that right?" I ask Mrs. Snippety Smith. She has been considering her situation and is ready to promise anything – even that she'll give me free chocolate for the rest of my life.

"Yes!" she cries.

Reluctantly, the V-kids open the cage and Mrs. Snippety Smith leaps out. They keep an eye on her, their fangs ready to taste a bit of witch blood if she makes a wrong move.

Released from her cage and ordeal, Mrs. Snippety Smith approaches me humbly, like I've never seen her before. She whispers into my ear, "Did you travel through the galaxy too?"

I nod and take her to a remote corner of the Cathedral. Red, Waltz, and the V-kids follow us with their eyes. Seeing that the witch hasn't turned me – or them – into anything, they withdraw into the Fortunes' kitchen.

Mrs. Snippety Smith tells me how – flying on her broom – she followed Mayor Icelandia de Winter's car on the streets of Salem. When she saw Mayor Icelandia de Winter holding me blindfolded in her car, she suspected the mayor was a wicked witch who snatched little girls like her daughter and delivered them to her kin by the Black Hollow Lake.

"Besides. . ." She pauses and stares into my eyes. "I promised your mother. . ."

"Mother? What did you promise her?"

"Marigold, I promised your mother I'd take care of you."

By the Salem witches' wands! Mrs. Snippety Smith, my guardian witch?

She says it happened a long time ago, during Halloween, on a week-long eclipse. Mother and Mrs. Snippety Smith were fighting Queen Nocturna, who had burst out of the Land of Endless-Night accompanied by the wicked witches. Mrs. Snippety Smith was leading her warrior witches battalion when a poisonous arrow hit her in the chest.

"Here." She shows me a terrible scar by the heart. "I thought I was going to die." She wipes a few tears and tells me Mother promised her that if she died, Mother would take care of Narcissa, her daughter, the same way Mrs. Snippety Smith would have to take care of me if Mother ever died. "But in the end your mother healed me with mandragora."

I'm crying together with Mrs. Snippety Smith. No Mother magic shell, no Mr. D! And this Transcarpathia seems such a faraway and unreachable place. It's already Tuesday noon. Will I ever find my relative?

"I followed you in the Ghostly-Trees Forest," Mrs. Snippety Smith continues, "and dropped my shawl over your head. I hoped I'd stop you from entering the Land of Endless-Night. I didn't know it was a Magic Corridor."

Brushing at her hair and tattered clothes with trembling hands, she explains that she had followed me through the pine's door, met Scorpio who terrified her and Sagittarius who mocked her, then chased her through the galaxy and pushed her in a bottomless black hollow. She fell for minutes, then what seemed like hours. Finally, she dropped like a boulder onto the ground of the Mute Woods, "where the little barbarians got me."

Mrs. Snippety Smith looks broken and exhausted. Although I know how mean she used to be to girls like me, I have to remember that nobody cooks better chocolate than she does.

"And there's more . . ." she says.

"Is everything all right here?" Red asks, approaching with Rose.

"Yes," I say, introducing Red and Rose to Mrs. Snippety Smith, who seems to be getting used to dealing with the fanged kids.

In her plump left hand Rose holds the painting of a tree bearing the name "mother," which she wants to show to "the ugly lady."

"Listen here," Mrs. Snippety Smith says. "I know these Black Suits."

"What?" Red says.

"I know their smell," Mrs. Snippety Smith says with a mysterious voice.

"That filthy, dead bug smell?" I ask.

"Yes. That's Queen Nocturna's smell."

"*Queen Nocturna*?" I say.

Mrs. Snippety Smith tells us that Queen Nocturna from the Land of Endless-Night can take various forms, can imitate other creatures and humans, animals and witches. It's said that after being defeated in the great Ash River Wars, Queen Nocturna spread all over the world.

"There's evil everywhere. That's what humans, animals, and witches have to fight against – "

"Queen Nocturna – " Red and I say together, flabbergasted.

"Your mother knew about this," Mrs. Snippety Smith says, searching into my eyes.

"Mother?"

"That's why she's dead." Mrs. Snippety Smith says with a confident voice. "You never thought she just vanished like green dust into thin air, did you?"

I stare at Red, whose dark blue eyes seem to be saying, "Told you!"

I fall on a dragon-shaped wooden chair, my mind a flurry of memories, my heart a dropping leaf.

By the Salem witches' wands! Queen Nocturna of the Land of Endless-Night killed Mother.

7. Voyage To the Sapphire Sea

Five blocks away from the Cathedral, Red, Waltz, and I sneak out of the sewers and walk into the North Railway Station.

The marble platform looks broken and deserted, like it's been through a bombardment. Shredded pages of newspaper flutter in the air, random bursts of wind reordering their messy piles. A few people dressed in gray dash to and from the platform, looking scared, like they're not supposed to be here. A long black train puffs choking clouds of steam.

Red says if we hurry we could catch the last car, sneak on, and hide under the benches, "where the conductor won't find us."

"But what if he does?" I ask.

Red grins. "We'll climb on the roof and run from economy class to first class."

Has he done this before?

I follow Red, who holds a muted Waltz under his coat. We tiptoe for a while, hiding behind pillars, afraid a Black Suits patrol might discover us. Occasionally we stumble on a piece of carved marble that once was part of the decoration of this railway station.

We reach the last car – there are twenty that make up the gloomy train. Nobody is looking, and we slip past the car's rear door into the cabin. We drop our trembling bodies onto the peeling gray benches.

"Waltz will keep an eye on the corridor," Red says – and sure enough, the poodle peeps into the hallway through the door's broken glass. After searching the cabin for the best hiding place, Red takes a seat under the window.

The locomotive jerks, pipes, and cracks so loud I'm afraid it'll lose all of its nails. I sit between Red and Waltz, happy that again I'm in Red's company. I've missed his jokes.

Darn, why am I blushing?

I'm grateful Red is gazing out the window, but I wish Waltz weren't throwing me an I-know-it look.

Just when I'm feeling discovered, we pass through a tunnel. The cabin suddenly turns pitch black. Darkness follows, and there's a kiss on my right cheek. My heart pounds and my head feels heavy. Waltz woofs, Red chuckles. Are they making fun of me?

When we're out in the light again, I ask Red, "Did you just kiss me?"

He doesn't answer. Instead he offers me a packet, which I unwrap to find a beautiful diary with cream pages that opens with a silver key.

"For you – to jot down memories of your time in Rondelia." He smiles, showing me his pearl-white fangs.

By the Salem witches' wands! Is it possible that Red really cares about me?

I check for Mother-the-hurtling-star, but all I see are Red's blue eyes reflected in the window.

We had to hide from the conductor twice under the benches and once hanging outside from the last car's door. And that's because I was so terrified by how quickly the villages and stations passed in front of our window that I refused to climb on the car's roof while the train ran full speed.

After three hours and two-hundred-and-fifty miles, we arrive at the Sapphire Sea railway station. We sneak out of the train and walk along streets paved with silver scales, smelling of fish. Spread over roofs, fish nets dripping sea water dry in the sun, and everywhere pelicans nest and scare away cawing seagulls.

Waltz sniffs around, hoping to find some leftover fish, while the streets of this place they should have called Smelly Fish City slowly take us toward the Museum of Archeology.

"Are we going in?" I ask, curious about the aquamarine building that looks like a giant seashell.

"Yep! That's where Zelda said we should start looking for the Time Gate." Red brushes at his clothes, licks his right hand, and mashes his hair against the scalp to look "like a real gentleman." He winks at me and looks from my torn jeans to my face.

"What?" I ask.

"You're pretty, did you know that?" Red says, smiling.

I pretend to look for Meow all over my "I ? Salem" T-shirt. "Have you seen my cat?"

"She's right here," he says. He approaches my left shoulder, points his index finger to my sleeve, bends his head, and steals another kiss from my cheek.

My face is on fire. I look up to search for Mother in the sky, but Red grabs my hand and off we go through the museum's revolving door. The door spins me in but holds Waltz hostage for an extra couple of turns. Red takes the whirl gleefully.

Ancient Greek and Roman statues surround us: a marble-draped Venus, a disc-throwing athlete, armor-clad emperors holding scepters and papyri edicts. Everywhere there are rusted metal helmets, mango-shaped amphorae, and Byzantine mosaics of kings with jeweled crowns.

After I've seen one too many ancient statues in marble cloaks, I get visions that the statues may be alive. I tell Red about it and he teases me, pretending that the ferocious head of Medusa Gorgona with her hundred hair-serpents has just bitten him and he's dying.

The museum's guide shows up behind a statue with a helmet that looks like a warrior witch and is labeled Palace Athena. Clear eyes light the woman's face, which reminds me of someone though I can't recall whom.

"Red, do you know that woman?"

"What woman?" Red asks from behind the statue of a sea-serpent god called Pontos, at the base of which Waltz sniffs and grimaces.

"The one over there."

Red heads boldly for the guide and says, "Excuse me, ma'am, do you have the time?"

"Why, certainly," the woman says, glancing at her watch. "It's half past – " She stops and stares at Red.

Red and the guide-woman stand mute, frozen, gazing at each other. Waltz gets nervous and woofs around the hall.

Has some strange magic turned them into statues?

I approach them, but they're in a trance. Red starts to shake, then the woman starts shaking too.

By the Salem witches' wands! What's going on?

Red collapses. The woman collapses, squashing Waltz under her falling weight. The poodle ultimately wriggles out from under her, yelping.

Red comes back to his senses. Tears fill his eyes. "Marigold," he says with a faint voice, "I think I've just found my mother."

"You *what*?"

"I think this woman is my mother," Red says, getting slowly to his feet. "I remember her eyes."

The woman looks confused. When at last she manages to stand up, she brushes off her gray skirt, stares at Red, and says, "Adrian, is it really you?"

"Uh . . . I guess. But they call me Red."

The woman says, "No, no, you're Adrian."

Waltz sniffs her silk stockings.

"You're twelve, right?" she asks.

Red nods.

Again there's silence. The two glance at each other, afraid to spell out that they are mother and son.

"I'm Lacrima," the woman says, her eyes filling with tears. She takes Red by the shoulders, calls him "Adrian again," and guides him over to a Roman marble bench, babbling questions that must have waited for more than a decade.

Waltz is coiled at Red's feet purring like a cat, staring at the woman with moist eyes, like he's found his lost mother as well.

Red has forgotten all about me. Although I'm happy for him – and shocked by what just happened – all of a sudden I feel gloomy, left behind, lost again in this odd country. And the autumn equinox is in just five days!

Listlessly I walk among the statues of ancient deities – Aphrodite and Apollo, Hermes and Hades, Hera and Zeus. As slow, sweet teardrops flow down my cheeks, I'm struck that Zelda knew about Red's mother. That's why she guided us to the Museum first. But has Red told his mother that he's a vampire?

All of a sudden there are loud voices. I run for the Roman marble bench, where an agitated Red and his mother stare at the turning door.

A dozen Black Suits glare at us.

"Follow me," Lacrima says.

We dash through halls and among statues until we reach the Great Tomb Hall, where we take refuge behind a statue of emperor Justinian.

"A secret cave that leads into the Sapphire Sea opens inside that sarcophagus," Lacrima says, pointing at an ancient coffin made of stone. "Hurry! When you reach the sea you'll have to swim to a small island, where you'll find a dinghy. Row until you reach the Turquoise River Delta, eighty miles from here. Only there will you be safe."

I'll be dead before we reach the Turquoise River Delta – I can't paddle for one mile, much less eighty. And what about the Time Gate?

Red keeps peering over his shoulder.

Waltz barks – furiously, like a bulldog.

"I'm not moving an inch." Red shows his fangs. "I'm staying here to protect you," he says to his mother.

Seeing Red's fangs, Lacrima steps back, trembling.

So Red hasn't yet revealed his vampire nature to her, probably afraid he might lose her. But now is not the time for confessions.

Heavy steps approach the Great Tomb Hall. I jump in the open sarcophagus and land on the sandy ground under the museum. Waltz drops on my knapsack, yelping.

"Don't be afraid of Red," I yell to Lacrima from below. "It's a long story – "

Bang! The sarcophagus's stone lid closes over my head.

We've been walking in darkness under the museum, when Waltz and I reach a place where the cave opens like a whale's mouth into the Sapphire Sea. A translucent sky pinned with spongy clouds stretches over the sea's rhythmic waves.

I get a bad feeling about diving into the sea – I hate having to bathe in cold water. I dip my left toes in and to my surprise find the water bearably tepid.

Waltz looks at me and says, "You're spoiled."

"Can you swim?" I ask, pretending I didn't hear him.

"Woof," Waltz says, then leaps into the water like he's been swimming in oceans all his life.

I have no excuse. I'll have to jump in, dressed and with my knapsack hanging on my back – which means everything in it will get soaked.

Here I go! I swim until the museum behind us turns small, like a real seashell. My body is warm from the effort. I've slurped a mouthful or two of salty water. It's getting dark. And where's that island?

Suddenly a fin that looks like a shark's, not ten feet away from me, rises above the water – and it keeps coming.

"Waltz!" I cry, frantically thrashing.

Something huge and silky brushes against my right palm. Although it's a pleasant tactile feeling, I'm terrified at the thought that it's a shark. The silky creature glides under my right armpit and propels me to the surface, just when I feel I'll surely drown. My head is out. I'm desperate to breathe air.

Waltz stares at me. When I peek under my arm, instead of a hideous teeth-filled mouth, I see the light-blue head of a dolphin.

"And the shark?" I ask Waltz.

"What shark?" Waltz says, sipping foam. "There're only dolphins around here. Sharks live in the middle of the sea, and they're not that big, either."

By the Salem witches' wands! I still have a chance to reach Transcarpathia and find my relative – assuming we discover the Time Gate and rescue Mr. D.

"Better give me a helping hand here," Waltz says, seeing me so comfortably carried by the dolphin.

The two of us ride on the dolphin's strong back, which shines with a luster of water and sunlight. We reach an algae-covered island no bigger than a merry-go-round. The dolphin leaves us on the shore.

I thank it from the bottom of my heart. It has saved me not only from a swim I could never make but also from a terrible death – if Waltz was wrong about the sharks.

I peel off my soggy jeans and my "I ? Salem" T-shirt. From my knapsack I pour out and scatter on the beach the pink and yellow bandanas I haven't lost yet and the spell vials. How fortunate it is that I left Meow at the Cathedral to be shampooed at the magic laundry – I would have killed my poor cat, drowning it in the Sapphire Sea.

I lie like a starfish on the beach and loll under the scorching sun. What's Red doing? Is he safe? What about his mom? Has he defeated the Black Suits?

"Why don't you check for the dinghy under those algae?" Waltz says, looking up from licking his paws.

I've no desire to budge from my splendid spot, but with a sigh I stand up, brush the sand off my skin, and head for the bushes, oozing a stench of putrefied algae.

"Can't find it," I say after the smell gets too strong.

Waltz, who has followed me all along, says, "Told you, you're spoiled – is that the best you can do?"

"Why don't you look for it?" I say, dropping on a sand dune.

"Listen!" Waltz woofs. "You lost Mr. D and now we're stranded in this God-forsaken place, with the Black Suits ready to show up any time."

"And what do you want me to do?"

"This is the Underground, not some girls' club, so keep looking."

Now I'm being dressed down by a dog. I throw a fistful of sand at Waltz – which misses him as a sea breeze blows the sand in all directions except his.

Muttering and with my back already red from sunburn, I search the thorny shrubs, poking through dead smelly algae.

"It's here!" I yell, scaring away some dragonflies.

The sand-colored dinghy is moored in algae and silt. But I have no problem dragging it out and dropping it in the sea. I grab my half-dried clothes from the beach and jump in the dinghy, stirring a few small waves around it.

Waltz arches and tries to leap straight in. But since he's just a small poodle with a big mouth, he misses the boat by half an inch and falls into the water.

Girls' club, hey?

"Get me out," Waltz woofs, giving me a baleful look.

Before he drowns – in anger if not the sea – I pull him out. As we're exchanging hostile glances, I notice that the dinghy has no oars, though odd-looking algae-made harnesses hang down into the water on both sides.

Could the dolphin know anything about this?

But there are only endless sheets of water around us under the orange afternoon sky.

Wait a minute. The dinghy moves gently and shakes. My first thought again is of sharks. But the dolphin's head shows up in front of us, then two pairs of opal-blue dolphins follow it. They fetch the harnesses in their muzzles, and off we glide through the Sapphire Sea's waves.

8. The Sea Dragon

$\mathcal{W}e$'ve been speeding through the Sapphire Sea, the wind fingering my hair. Waltz whistles an eerie poodle carol, glaring at me as he stands on the bottom of the dinghy, small, his fur wild, his face full of spite.

How can I make peace with him?

I dip my thumb in the water. To my surprise, it bumps into something solid but slippery. I don't catch it, whatever it was.

As I look back, an object glows in the sun. What could it be? Maybe I've just missed a bottle that holds the map to a lost pirate treasure. Wouldn't it be nice to wear its glimmering pearl necklaces, emerald bracelets, ruby earrings, and diamond crowns?

But something again shines ahead. It's a brilliant blue stone. I thrust my hand in the water and catch it.

"Waltz, look here! What's this?"

Waltz barely turns his snooty poodle head and says, "Anybody can see it's an uncut sapphire. This *is* the Sapphire Sea, you know."

"I do know, but I thought it was called that because of its blue color."

"Not really." Waltz explains that at times sapphires of various sizes and shades show up in the sea's waves, though nobody knows exactly why.

Another stone pops up in the water. I catch it, and another one emerges on the crest of a wave. A trail of sapphires floats on the water, stretching all the way to the horizon, as if they were a road of gems leading to the other side of the planet.

"Look!" Waltz is peering at the line where aquamarine-blue sea meets opalescent sky.

Suddenly the horizon line quivers – growing into coils that move half in water, half in air – and turns toward us, heading straight for our dinghy.

Waltz and I freeze.

As it approaches we realize it's not the horizon, it's a giant sea dragon! And that's not all. What's just as extraordinary is that the reptile glows in the sunlight like it's on fire, although the blaze it spreads is intensely blue.

The dolphins carrying us suddenly stop and align on either side of the boat. They bounce in the air, then dive, as if bowing respectfully to the creature ahead. My dolphin friend blinks at me, flapping its fin like it's saying goodbye. Then the five of them are gone, leaving us in these strange waters while a huge sea dragon curls through the waves, closing in on us.

All my fears return. I feel doomed and alone, lost with a grumpy poodle in the middle of a sea that bears the name of a beautiful gem but is deadly and dangerous, with a hundred-foot-long sea dragon poised to kill me.

When the gleaming blue sea dragon eventually reaches us, Waltz and I are on the verge of collapsing.

Mr. Londinium Oxford's face pops up in my mind. I wish he were here to witness that I, Marigold, the last herbs witch of Salem, before dying, saw a giant sea dragon like the ones he only drew from his imagination.

As I look at the sea dragon more carefully, I realize its shining skin isn't a skin at all. Its entire body is covered with blue gemstones.

"Sapphires," Waltz whispers.

The sea dragon oozes an aromatic scent like camphor, which I find surprisingly pleasant, considering that I'm about to die. It sniffs our dinghy and zips out a forked blue tongue. It licks Waltz, then my face. I cringe. Who is it going to eat first? I close my eyes, waiting.

But nothing happens.

When I open my eyes, its front half is coiled around our dinghy and its back half rumples the sea with concentric water creases.

But the sea dragon is blind. Instead of eyes, it has two deep holes.

"Where are its eyes?" I ask Waltz.

The sea dragon hears me, lifts its huge head, and hums.

Waltz leaps in front of me – quite heroically, I'd say – and hums back at the sea dragon.

I didn't know Waltz could speak other creatures' languages.

The two hum at each other: the sea dragon ever so somberly – constantly shedding sapphires into the sea, where they melt in dark blue stains, Waltz ever so high-pitched, waving his tail.

Suddenly the humming stops. Waltz turns to me and says, "Don't be afraid. Say 'hi' to the Sapphire Sea Dragon, the King of Sapphire Sea"

"Hello," I say in a hoarse voice. "I'm Marigold, and I've come all the way from Salem."

The sea dragon nods at me, its purple-blue head glowing in the twilight.

Waltz says the sea dragon-king has just told him that it has been living here since the time when the sea was just a small lake of sapphires and water. A thousand years ago, when the rains filled the whole valley and turned the lake into a sea, the

Sapphire Sea Dragon was declared king by all that lived underwater: algae, plankton, dolphins, sharks, octopuses, jellyfish, seahorses, sea anemones, and mermaids. It has always lived happy and gleaming – a true king of the sea – shedding its sapphire scales for the water to melt the gems and dye its waves with blue shades.

Until one day when the Black Suits caught it and took out its eyes, the biggest sapphire gems in the world. But as they prepared to harvest the rest of the precious stones from its skin, the king escaped – rescued by a band of pirates who lived on Snakes Island, a few miles away in the Turquoise River Delta.

"And the sea dragon-king will take us there," Waltz says, woofing joyfully.

When the sky turns to a blaze of red, the Sapphire Sea Dragon carries our dinghy further north. We reach an island covered in reeds, willows, wicker, and seashells.

With the tip of its sapphire tail, the sea dragon pushes our dinghy onto the beach. It climbs on a sand dune next to me and wraps its coils around a foam-bleached coral, its blue shades in the twilight creating a silvery reflection in the sky.

I feel sadness and awe at the sight of this beautiful creature the Black Suits have mutilated. Maybe one day when I become a herbs witch, I'll find a magic potion to restore its sight.

There's a familiar hissing, and Zelda shows up from the wicker-thick depths of the island.

"Hello, Marigold!" she says.

"Is it really you?" I ask. I've never been happier to see a vampire.

But something stuck in the beach distracts me – a black flag with a human skull.

"What is this island?" I ask Zelda.

"It's Snakes Island, Simon-Sea-Phantom's island – "

"Simon-Sea-Phantom?"

"Yes. He's a pirate, and so are his chums."

Pirates? What about the treasures I dreamed of earlier?

"They're still at large now," Zelda says, "checking for the Time Gate."

My sunburnt face lights up. So it's true! There is a Time Gate in the Sapphire Sea. I fall on a sand dune, tired and amazed. Waltz scowls at me. My eyes still swimmy from the Sapphire Sea Dragon's bluish-black sparks, I fall asleep. I dream that I heroically vanquish the Black Suits and get the King of the Sea its precious sapphire eyes back.

Simon-Sea-Phantom and his six-pirate band pull their ship to the shore. They throw a party in my honor, which they spice with pirate stories from the Opal, Ruby, Jade, and Zirconium seas and oceans they've sailed through.

I'm lying around a fire that fries all sorts of round, cubic, and rhombic fish I've never seen before. I'm comfortable in a warm bed of sand.

Simon-Sea-Phantom is the first pirate I've met in my life. His right hand has seven fingers. He uses his extra index to swing cards like straws and to better grab bottles of wine. With his extra pinky, he twists against his thumb the edges of his black mustache. His voice is hoarse, his hair is thick and curly, and he wears a black patch on his left eye.

"Five years ago the Black Suits kidnapped our children," Simon-Sea-Phantom says. "That's why we've become pirates." But the Black Suits are furious because they can't catch the pirates even when they chase their boat down to the Bosphorus Straits. Vampires like Zelda and the V-kids warn the pirates ahead of time about the Black Suits' attacks. "Occasionally they defend us with a bite or two."

Unfortunately, this vampire-pirate alliance made the Black Suits realize that a secret organization is working against them: Mr. D's Underground made up of grown-up vampires, V-kids, Roma magicians, time travelers, and pirates. And these days the Black Suits' surveillance over the Underground is tougher than ever, day and night. "But don't you worry," Simon-Sea-Phantom says. "One day we'll beat them for good, mark my pirate word!"

Simon-Sea-Phantom says we're going out to rescue Mr. D. Midnight is the only time when the water Time Gate opens "for one long minute. Then, puff -- it's gone." He pulls out a sphere from under his left pirate eye patch. "Check this out, kiddo."

It's horrible! How can I touch his left eyeball?

"Courage, kiddo," he says, grinning. "It's Roma magic crystal."

A strange world of colors revolves inside the eyeball. Red and orange, then blue and green, finally ashy and black.

"It's a gift from Zaraza," Simon-Sea-Phantom says. "It shows me whatever my eyes can't see and my imagination can't picture." And this eyeball showed the pirates where the water Time Gate is, "between the Mermaids' Cave and the Octopus Cliff – five miles eastward."

We're sailing through the foggy waters in a twenty-foot-long boat. The air feels heavy with waiting. The moon sheds soft beams over the fog. Our boat floats through the whirling vapors like a phantom.

A pirate who lost his left leg below his knee – and uses a cedar branch instead – says the Mermaids' Cave isn't too far away from Snakes Island. "They're pretty nasty," he says. The sirens woo sailors into their cave, feed them delicious poisonous meals, and offer their corpses to their friends the fish and the seahorses.

By the Salem witches' wands! They're nastier than the wicked witches.

I'm getting cold.

At midnight a gust of wind pierces the fog. It gets stronger, until it blows away all the mist. Stranded in a ghostly boat, we're connected by a strange magic with the Sapphire Sea and the hurtling star above.

"Here it comes," a hunchbacked pirate says, pointing at the separating waters.

"The water Time Gate," another says.

Wave after wave, the waters sink into a cocoon of foam. We're five feet away and keep paddling backward.

The cocoon turns into a crater of waters that disappear, roaring, into a mass of waterfalls.

"What's that?" I ask, pointing at a giant tentacle emerging from the vortex's center.

"Lads!" Simon-Sea-Phantom yells. "It's the darn octopus again!"

"What's that?" I ask, frantic as more tentacles rise up.

"A giant squid with a hundred arms," a red-haired pirate yells at me over the blasting sound of the falling waters. "It's got our boat more than once."

Just as the waters open and a hideous octopus head rises a foot above our boat, Simon-Sea-Phantom whips out a bottle and sprinkles the contents over the creature's head.

"Take this," he says, "and don't you get drunk now, girl." He laughs.

"What's he doing?" I ask.

"Seasoning her with vinegar," the maimed pirate says. "This one octopus loves it so much, she'll forget about our ship. See?"

The others laugh.

I don't.

After the octopus sinks back in the vortex, burping, a hand with elongated yellowish fingers sticks out of the whirlpool.

By the Salem witches' wands!

The pirates get ready to lift a half-undead Mr. D into the boat. But the octopus is back! She thrusts tentacles toward Mr. D, hoping to ensnare him, her mouth open.

She must be drunk, not to realize that this is a vampire.

Simon-Sea-Phantom is out of vinegar. The pirates panic.

Should I use a Roma spell from Zaraza?

As I search through my backpack, our boat is thrown back. I cling to its oars, hoping I won't fall in the stormy waters.

What was that? Another octopus?

No. A glittering blue sea-dragon head attacks the mollusk.

The Sapphire Sea Dragon!

It blasts its coils into the octopus's tentacles, then bites its head. The octopus smashes the waves with some of its arms, others it sends onto the sea dragon, trying to choke it. Although blind, the Sapphire Sea Dragon is still powerful. It cuts the octopus's skin with its gems, and the octopus is forced to withdraw. Still dizzy from the vinegar and hurt, the mollusk retires in the depths of the waters, just as the Time Gate closes back.

And Mr. D?

He's floating, shivering, his face livid, thrusting a cadaverous hand toward our boat.

"And up you go," Simon-Sea-Phantom says, while the pirates pull and lift Mr. D in.

A drenched Mr. D says the drunken octopus scared him pretty badly. He sneezes and swears that the lost city of Atlantis lies at the bottom of the Sapphire Sea – "back in time, of course." That's where he's been hiding ever since he escaped the Black Suits who chased him through the Time Corridor.

I haven't uttered a word yet. Can Mr. D forgive me for sending him into the time warp?

"Marigold," he finally says, "let me show you something." He pulls whatever it is out of his cloak but keeps it hidden in his hand.

"Mr. D," I say, looking at my torn jeans, "I'm sorry . . . "

"Here," he says, as if he didn't hear me. He opens his fist.

Shining in the moonlight, the most beautiful scarlet seashell lies in his palm.

"Take it," Mr. D says, "it's yours. Now you won't have to worry about finding the other one."

In seconds he's asleep on the bottom of the boat, jerking, sodden, his eyelids ticking nervously. And I take it that Mr. D and I are friends again, even if I lost him for a while back in time, even if this shell isn't magical but a precious gift.

9. Transcarpathia

On Wednesday before sunrise the pirates leave us on the northern shore of the Sapphire Sea. Again we enter the Enchanted Forest.

Mr. D has turned into a lizard. We encounter a few Roma kids who pick up mushrooms. Mr. D approaches them as fast as a full-speed train, and the children jump aside. They catch up with us, but only for a second. No one is a match for Mr. D-the-lizard – let alone a kid. They holler behind us, imitating monkeys, dogs, wolves, owls.

We jump into a stream Mr. D calls the Clear-Water River. He floats like an alligator while I sit on his back, afraid I might fall in the water – which strikes me as anything but clear. In fact, small puddles of oil float on top of it, and a few dead fish drift belly-up with their mouths opened, their eyes turned inside out.

"What's wrong with the river?" I ask.

"The Black Suits have polluted it," Mr. D says. "You could hardly imagine how clear this water used to be." He swallows a mouthful and spits it out, trying to keep his chin above the dirty surface.

Out of nowhere, a toad hops on his back, shamelessly croaking.

"Take it off me!" Mr. D yells. "I hate frogs."

I thrust my right arm toward the wretched creature, which has landed right on Mr. D's tail. But no matter what I do I can't grasp it or scare it off. I stretch and stretch until my left hand slides. To my horror, I fall into the stinking river.

"Help! Get me out of here!" I'm approaching a big dead ugly fish.

Mr. D grabs me with his claws and throws me on his back. I'm soaked, angry, and dirty. Very dirty. The toad is gone, and it did well for I would've tried one of Zaraza's magic spells on it, turning it into a. . .but what's uglier than a frog?

I'm drying out, lying on Mr. D's back. I nap for a while. When I wake up, we're swimming in a crystalline stream up in the mountains. Mr. D lands in the evergreen woods, "at the border with Transcarpathia," he says, "and five miles from Castle Bran."

We're in a meadow with canopy wagons that look familiar.

"The Roma painters live in these woods," Mr. D says. He needs to rest at their camp, and more importantly, to hide from the sun until dusk.

When they emerge from the forest, the Romas say Zaraza sent them word through the messenger leaves that we'd drop by their camp. They tell us about their art of painting angels and dragons on monastery walls. They even show us how to make secret colors out of leaves, wax, grass, and petals.

"These colors last forever. You want to see?" says a Roma painter kid who has invited me into his tent. He shows me crystal cans filled with colors bearing strange names: "oreen," a mixture of orange and green, "redet," a mixture of red and violet, "fublue," a mixture of fuchsia and blue, and "yellet," a mixture of yellow and scarlet.

"Can you draw me something?" I ask him.

He takes some oreen and fublue, and wielding the brush like a sword, paints a butterfly with a dozen wings. When it's ready, the butterfly takes off from the canvas, its wings wet and shimmering. As it flies, it scatters droplets of color throughout the tent, then outside, staining the grass and even the air, until it disappears into the woods.

At sunset we're back on the road, at the border with Transcarpathia.

"How will we pass through the checkpoint?" I ask Mr. D, worried about the Black Suits.

"Through the Bears' Cave, this way."

Suddenly a Black Suits patrol peers at us from the gated border.

Mr. D-the-lizard ducks and turns green, head to toe, like the grass. "The cave crosses right under the border between Rondelia and Transcarpathia," he whispers, crawling through the underbrush. "There's an exit at its far end, under a boulder – a hole that opens straight into a meadow in Transcarpathia."

"Are there any bears in here?" I ask as we reach the cave.

"They're all dead. The Black Suits have hunted them down."

We enter the dim cave. Stumps and roots pierce the ceiling, allowing silver spears of moonlight to filter inside. The strong smell of wet cedar wood – probably from the trees above – spreads throughout the cavern. The floor is littered with large skeletons that once sustained the bodies of bears.

Something moves at the back of the cavern. Mr. D and I stare at the little black mass, which changes position in the dark. A creature makes a noise that's part whine, part muffled roar. As we get closer, we distinguish a ball of fur tumbling at the back of the cave: a brown bear cub.

Upon seeing us, it freezes. Then it resumes whine-roaring even louder, the sound resonating throughout the entire cavern if not the entire woods.

"We've got to get out of here – fast!" Mr. D says.

"Why?"

"Because this cub must have a mother, and mama bears are fearsome fighters when they think their cubs are in danger."

"But you said there were no bears left – "

"Who knows where these two might have come from to take refuge here?"

Mr. D searches for the boulder at the back of the cavern, right where the cub is making more noise than ever. Just as he finds it, we hear heavy steps behind us, followed by a terrible growl.

There's no point in asking Mr. D what the noise is. He frantically tries pushing the boulder aside, but it isn't budging. I rush to press my hands on the mass of stone – we heave together, more and more desperate as the growling gets closer.

No, I won't panic! I keep pushing the darn rock. Again. And again.

By the time the boulder jerks with a creepy screech on the stony floor, we're exhausted and breathless. But we've actually moved it aside.

A massive paw with huge claws swoops from behind, missing me by only half an inch but touching my hair and swiping my last bandana. Before it can muster another swoop, Mr. D and I are out -- in a meadow, gulping fresh mountain air.

The mama bear's terrible roar is behind us.

We don't stop until we reach another meadow, at the foot of a cliff "on the Green Peeks Mountains," as Mr. D explains. On the cliff looms a castle -- gigantic, dark, and mysterious.

"Marigold, at last – this is Castle Bran," he says.

The castle's brick walls, its high towers and turrets, its arrow loops and eye-shaped windows leave me no doubt as to its reputation as a fortress.

A dark yellow cloud passes before the moon, leaving us in darkness. A shiver travels my backbone. When the moon returns, it throws a pale light on a well right in the midst of the glade.

The scare with the bear has left me thirsty. I approach the well, but Mr. D is quicker. He struggles with the well's heavy wooden lid. When he finally pushes the lid aside, I don't see any water – only walls covered with moss.

"Please get in," Mr. D says.

"What?"

"Don't be afraid. It's not that deep, only six feet." Mr. D explains that upon reaching the bottom of the well, I'll find an entry to a narrow tunnel leading to an old elevator that goes further down, to some mines in the belly of the mountain. "Wait for me by the elevator, all right?"

What's an elevator doing in a medieval castle?

Halfheartedly, I climb into the empty well and drop to the ground. I bring my feet together and try in vain to see what's around me – it's pitch-black everywhere. Blindly I touch the soggy floor and the sticky walls. After a few moves, I feel the rim of an opening. I crouch and creep mole-style along a narrow tunnel, advance slowly until I reach an expanse of cold metal. Can this be the elevator?

Are my eyes getting a bit used to the darkness? There's a loud thud behind me. Mr. D swears in a foreign language – Transcarpathian? – and groans. He's fallen and is lying on his back, his legs pointing up. I can't stop a muffled giggle.

Mr. D hears me, coughs as if he's embarrassed, turns over, and crawls toward me through the tunnel. As he gets closer, I freak out. In the dark, Mr. D's eyes glow yellow, the pupils shrinking vertically like a cat's.

"So," he says, " a bit of light is of real help now, don't you think?"

"Absolutely," I say. After all, no matter how nice he is, Mr. D is a vampire.

He brings his body near me, and his eyes light up the area around us.

The elevator is just a rusted cage of bars and one button shoved into the ceiling. We push it, and the corroded contraption bolts. We descend into the abyss, the elevator squeaking and rocking like it's going to fall any second.

At the bottom of the mountain, the tunnels stretch like crossroads. We're taking the right passage, which Mr. D says mounts to the castle's rooms.

As we're walking through the mine, I decide to ask him, "Mr. D, now that we're here in Transcarpathia, do you think it'll take long before I find my relative? You know, it's already Wednesday night – "

"I know, Marigold," he says with a serious voice. "Don't you worry. In five centuries I've never broken a promise."

Mr. D explains that it was the Cavaliers of the Teutonic Order who built the castle in 1212. At the end of the thirteenth century, the Saxons from Transcarpathia took it over.

"I got Bran from the Saxons," he says. "Once my body got older, I added the elevator in the well. I needed it for my nightly dining visits down in the village."

While he goes on to brag about the wars he fought with the Turks, Tartars, Mongols, and Furry-Hats invaders, a little thought keeps bugging me. It's those nightly dining visits he mentioned. Did he mean sucking the blood of the villagers?

"When I moved to Bookrest," Mr. D says, "I left Bran as a gift to Transcarpathia. I heard they kept it in a pretty good shape. It's a museum now, you know. . . ."

I can't tell how long we've been walking in the mine that keeps slanting upward steeply. At the end of a tunnel, we reach a door covered with bark.

Mr. D smashes his body into it, and the door creaks open with a screech of rusted hinges. We're in yet another tunnel, but by the looks of its painted walls and lit candles, this must be a corridor inside the castle.

We climb a dozen steps and open another door into what Mr. D says is the Council Room.

The chamber is furnished with nothing but a heavy oak table covered with maps, blueprints, and documents in foreign languages. The Dragon sign – Mr. D's emblem – and two crossed swords hang from a wall above a fireplace.

All of a sudden the swords hop off the wall and onto the wooden floor. They point their blades' tips toward us, ready to attack.

"Sword to your left," I yell at Mr. D.

"Thanks," he says, ducking as a silver sword whizzes above his head.

The sword retreats and pairs with its golden twin. The two attack Mr. D from left and right – but he's quicker and crouches, while they cross their glinting blades, snipping his left ear.

Mr. D gets to his feet, holds his left hand over his ear, and with his right hand catches the flying swords by their blades. He smashes them on the floor. When the swords try to rise again, he holds them hostage under his feet.

"Don't you recognize me?" he yells at the swords.

The swords turn inanimate.

"You," Mr. D says, pointing at the silver blade. "You were my best friend during the battles I won in the sixteenth century, don't you remember?"

The silver sword jerks under his right foot.

"And you," Mr. D says, addressing the golden sword, "I chopped off heads with you in the seventeenth century, have you forgotten?"

The golden sword twists.

Mr. D gently lifts his feet off the blades, and the swords rise and pair in front of him like soldiers. They bow and cross three times, clacking, after which they resume their position on the wall, under Mr. D's Dragon sign.

"That's more like it." Mr. D sounds like exactly what he is: a master who has finally returned home.

The fire in the hearth plays strange shadows on the now quiet walls. Something moving on my left suddenly draws my attention.

Mr. D's elongated shadow quivers above the fireplace: Here are his gargoyle nose and right ear, his sharp chin and long fingers. The shadow glides and stops in the middle of the room. By the Salem witches' wands! It has a life of its own.

I peek at my own small shadow, quivering behind me like a scared mouse. Mr. D's could be a separate creature. In Salem our shadows don't walk by themselves – although they say the wicked witches of the Black Hollow Lake use strong black magic to split shadows from bodies.

Mr. D says with the most natural voice, as if everybody talked to their live shadows, "Mr. Shadow, could you please go ahead of us and check to see if all is clear?"

The shadow nods, whooshes onto another wall, curls over the table, the swords, and the blueprints, creeps on the floor, then it's out through the window. It coils like a serpent around roof ridges and flows forward on parapets.

When this unusual butler comes back, it makes mysterious signs with its fingers.

"No Black Suits, but the place is crawling with castle guards," Mr. D says.

He pushes a brick opposite the fireplace. The false wall spins. A secret door!

We take a narrow staircase down a dark hallway oozing with vanilla candles.

"My secret apartments," Mr. D says.

On my left, there's a kitchenette no bigger than a booth. A white piece of marble with black cobwebs and polished edges occupies most of the space inside. The stone is so beautiful I think it may have once served other purposes than a table in this castle. It would make a splendid fireplace decoration.

At the end of the corridor, we enter a room – the only one – which serves as living room, dining room, library, and bedroom. A secretaire with lots of little drawers and an ancient scarlet piano with a few keys missing are stacked on either side of a small oval-shaped window. Antique books with ragged leather covers, edges missing, and black stains suggesting they've been rescued from fire have been thrown at random in a floor-to-ceiling bookcase.

"Remnants of my old collection," Mr. D says, waving me into a reclining leather chair encrusted with red dragons.

Then I see the piece de resistance – a long black coffin with a dirty white satin-upholstered mattress. Can this be Mr. D's bed? And so it is. Mr. D jumps into the coffin, nestles his tall figure in its depths, and rests his head on a moth-eaten pillow. Although he's half sunk, his gargoyle nose sticks out of the coffin. He's bragging about the battles he won against the Furry-Hats Empire in the eighteenth century.

Comfortably installed in the recliner, I glance around the mildew-covered walls. Mr. D's portrait draws my attention first. The painter did a nice job, tinging his face and hands with a luster that makes him look almost angelic. Was he younger when he posed? The painting oddly resembles an El Greco purple brocade-clad cardinal I once saw in an art catalogue at the Salem Public Library of Witchcraft.

"Would you like a snack?" Mr. D asks me from the coffin-bed.

"Yes, please. I'd like something light, like fruits and a soda," I say, hoping that some of this might show up out of nowhere, as it would from the Cathedral's magic kitchen.

Mr. D bounds out of his coffin and heads for the kitchenette – apparently not everything around here operates on some kind of Roma or vampire witchcraft.

Mr. D searches through boxes, drops something metallic on the floor like a fork or a knife, spills a liquid, breaks a glass, then crashes into something, crying out in pain and swearing in Transcarpathian – which, again, I don't understand.

After a while he reappears, carrying a glass of milk and a plate of chocolate wafers. He offers them to me as if nothing has happened in the kitchenette and excuses himself for being out of provisions.

"You know, it's been a long time since I've been here," he says. With that he dives into the coffin, relieved that I'm not asking him to do anything else.

I sip then spit the milk. Is the milk from this century? I drop the wafers in my backpack. I'll eat them later.

Next to Mr. D's picture hangs the portrait of a woman painted in black. Below it, a small bronze plate reads: Marga, 1570. The woman has sad eyes. I have an odd feeling about her.

"Who is Marga?" I ask.

Mr. D pops his head out of the coffin and stares at me for a long moment. "She was my princess wife in the fifteen hundreds." He explains that when he became a vampire he wanted to have Marga with him forever. He gave her the kiss of death and turned her into a vampire. Marga lived for another hundred years or so before she mysteriously vanished in the forests surrounding Castle Bran.

"This portrait of hers was made right before her disappearance. She was pretty upset when she posed," Mr. D says. "She never really adjusted to a vampire's afterlife." He says that Marga thought living forever would bring unhappiness. She wanted to die like a human at seventy, or at eighty, or even at ninety. She hated being the undead, because she couldn't rest or dream. Later, when she had nowhere else to go, for she had already visited the world twice, she became melancholy and thought that living was meaningless. "She had a point." Mr. D sighs.

"What do you mean?"

"You see, time – past, present, future – means nothing to us, the undead, although we do feel time's presence and flow."

After they had searched for Marga in the woods of Transcarpathia, and upon his return to the castle, Mr. D found a letter and a rosebud on their princely canopy bed.

"The letter contained shocking news."

Mr. D leaps out of his coffin once more and begins a frenzied search through his secretaire. He throws out scraps, papers, and papyri with all sorts of astonishing drawings and blueprints: the Vampire Organ I saw at the Cathedral, a strange instrument with hundreds of strings, a contraption filled with pikes, a cage, a miniature castle, and a bat.

But he has trouble finding what he's looking for. He kicks the plans and models to the floor, then finally, upon jerking out and smashing the drawers, from the depths of the secretaire brings out a packet of letters tied with red ribbon.

His eyes filled with tears, he browses through the dusty letters. He pulls from an envelope a sheet of paper that looks so old it has become transparent and is practically illegible. Still, he unfolds it, takes a deep breath, and reads it to me.

Beloved,
I have decided to renounce my immortality.
I leave you this beautiful bud as a symbol of my undying love.
This rose will never blossom and my love for you will never die.
Yours forever,
Marga

Agate-red teardrops slip down Mr. D's cheeks.

I never imagined the passage of time could hurt so badly. By the Salem witches' wands! Wasn't eternal life supposed to bring happiness?

10. Dracula's Castle

I've slept dressed in my jeans and my "I ? Salem" T-shirt, with my shoes' laces hanging like a cat's whiskers and my hair spreading all over the knapsack I used for a pillow. I've slept without dreams or nightmares, as if my mind turned into a blank sheet of paper.

A brisk melody wakes me up. Where's Mr. D? His gargoyle nose isn't sticking out of his coffin-bed. I spot him at the piano and say, "Good morning."

He nods without raising his eyes from the keyboard.

"What are you playing?" I ask.

"Prokofiev's 'Peter and the Wolf.' It's a piece for kids, like you." He says I should listen to this musical tale, because it teaches children about the different instruments: the flute that plays the bird and the clarinet that plays the cat, the oboe that plays the duck and the timpani drums that play the hunter, the violins that play Peter and the French horns that play the wolf.

Just when I've gathered an entire orchestra in my mind, Mr. D says, "Want to see something?"

He pulls the silky cover off a birdcage the shape of a Japanese temple. Inside, the most beautiful white dove dozes, her head hidden behind a wing.

"My pet," Mr. D says. "At dusk she always comes back, at dawn she flies away – for centuries."

He takes the dove in his hand, caresses her beautiful feathers, and feeds her from his palm.

Who'd have thought that Mr. D would turn out to be one of the kindest people I've ever met – even if he's a vampire, even if he's Dracula?

"In an old bookshop in Ancient Books Street, hidden on a dusty shelf, I found one of my old books, a fifteenth-century treatise on the genealogy of the Draculas," Mr. D says, all dressed up in a cloak, red on either side, and an elegant black fedora.

The volume belonged to his extensive library from Castle Bran, which he'd taken with him to Bookrest when he moved to Rondelia. But when the Black Suits came to power, they confiscated many precious volumes. In spite of this, Mr. D hid and spread a few books – including this treatise – with the secret network of antiquarians. Now, since he's been out of the Prison of Tears, Mr. D has been tracking down his books throughout the libraries of Bookrest, often without success.

"Anyway, halfway through this treatise I found an astonishing prediction. It's said that when Dracula is joined by his last living descendant, and together they gear their efforts for the benefit of mankind, they'll be able to vanquish all that is evil, all that brings suffering to the people and the land."

I imagine a boy with shiny fangs and lots of guts, someone like Red, knocking at Mr. D's door, introducing himself as the last Dracula on the face of the earth.

"But it's been decades," Mr. D says with a sad voice, "and I've lost any hope."

We leave the secret apartments, then the Council Room through a door that opens into the Gothic Room.

This dark room is filled with a collection of paintings and small statues of gargoyles. What nasty grimaces! The weirdest thing is that all the gargoyles in this room have Mr. D's face – or variations of it – as if a crazy artist has tried to paint and sculpt the ugliest versions of Dracula.

Mr. D slaps his forehead. "Darn! How could I forget? Of course it's not here -- we've been going in the wrong direction. We need to go to the Music Room." With that, he vanishes through a door, leaving me in absolute darkness.

As I'm tiptoeing toward the door, something pinches the back of my neck, prickles the skin of my forearm, and slaps my left cheek. Other hands try to pull off my jeans. But there's only darkness around me.

"Help! Mr. D. . ."

Wherever he went, he can't hear me. I'm alone, under attack, and can't see my assailant.

I dash in circles through the room, yelling and hitting at random sculptures that crash with a terrible noise. Somebody or something keeps pushing and pinching and slapping me, until I'm cornered. It feels like a hundred paws have gotten hold of me. When they manage to throw me to the ground, something hissing into my ear, I figure this must be the end.

Still I keep fighting, hitting and squirming, trying to get loose. I search desperately through my backpack, hoping to find something – anything – to help me. Finally I take out the kaleidoscope and the firefly inside lights it up, scaring whatever or whoever was holding me hostage to the ground.

Humiliated but not hurt, I crawl behind a statue of Mr. D-the-gargoyle, clutching the kaleidoscope like it's the most important thing in my life. The whispers in the room get stronger and louder.

I raise the firefly-lit kaleidoscope up in the air to discover an entire population of gargoyle statues peering at me, licking their fangs, walking backward, afraid of the light. I might have become their supper, save for the lucky firefly Zaraza gave me in the Enchanted Forest.

The deadly little gargoyles keep their distance -- until the firefly bursts out of the kaleidoscope and flies through the room, lighting it at random like a tiny projector gone wild. The gargoyles panic and dash about aimlessly, colliding and smashing their marble heads.

When at last the firefly vanishes through a little bullet hole it finds in the stained-glass window, I'm alone and once again become the gargoyles' prey. Probably nobody leaves Transcarpathia alive!

The door breaks open and Mr. D makes a sudden glorious entrance, mortifying the little creatures that withdraw, hissing, into walls, paintings, and pedestals.

"Is everything all right in here?" Mr. D is gaping at my torn T-shirt and terrified face. "I thought I heard noise. Where were you?"

"I was here," I say, brushing off my jeans, shoving the kaleidoscope in my knapsack.

"Don't tell me those gargoyles dared attack you!"

I nod, exhausted, feeling bruises all over my body.

"One day I'll have to teach those little clowns a lesson," Mr. D says, lighting the room with his sinister eyes. "You know why?"

"Why?"

"Because they're only copies of me. They're not me. They can't act of their free will." He drags me out of the room while the gargoyles chuckle behind us. "At least, they're not supposed to," Mr. D says in a resigned voice.

Back through the Council Room, we take a secret staircase that squeaks all the way up to the second floor.

Suddenly there's a noise. Did the gargoyles dare follow us? No, these are human voices approaching in the dark. Mr. D stops his vigorous advance. I freeze.

"I tell you, I heard something," a man not far from us says. He sounds scared. Read here

"Bah! There's nothing in here. I've been guarding this castle for more than ten years. Aside from a pathetic ghost that sleeps in the Princely Dormitory, you won't find anybody – place has been quiet as a tomb ever since the kings left. Of course, we like to joke with the other guards, betting twenty bucks on who's going to bump into the vampire first." The man giggles, standing only a foot or so from us. "But I'm telling you, this whole Dracula thing is just a legend – "

"Enough!" Mr. D jumps right in front of the castle guards. In a bass maître d' voice he says, "Good evening, gentlemen! What can I do for you?"

At the terrible sight of Mr. D's cockeyed grin, revealing two bloodthirsty fangs, the guard who declared Dracula a legend slides to the floor. The other, whose face shows only one terrified eye, pees in his pants.

"Please, sir. Don't hurt me, please!" Walking backward, he hits the wall and staggers. He tries to stand up like a man but can't stop his knees from shaking.

"Boo!" Mr. D yells at him.

The castle guards turn and flee, screaming.

Mr. D and I laugh – with hiccups. When we finally stop, Mr. D says we need to hurry. "They might come back with more castle guards, and I'm not up for a fight."

Still on the second floor, we pass through the Princely Dormitory. The only piece of furniture there is a shell-shaped chestnut canopy bed. Blue sheets of brocade cover the bed, and the canopy is as transparent as if it were made of spider webs.

"I once spent a night in this bed," Mr. D says, "but I didn't like it at all – too spooky. I dreamed a ghost visited me."

Just as we're about to move into the next room, a whoosh comes from under the canopy. There's nothing to see, though, only the cobwebby fabric waving gently, as if a zephyr crossed through it. I leave the quiet room, anxious to check out the next one, which Mr. D calls the Oriental Room.

Piles of Persian, Indian, Chinese, and Japanese wool and silk rugs, diamond-shaped ivory tables, and elephant tusks decorate this room. Three wooden statues of gods and goddesses dancing on pedestals twist, turn, and wave their legs and arms.

"These are live reproductions of Buddha, Shiva, Brahma, and Vishnu – they're Indian gods." Mr. D tells me about the faraway lands of East India and its magic ways. He visited Delhi at the end of the last century and took breathing lessons from a yoga master "to help ease my advanced age." He was stunned when the yoga teacher revealed that he was older than Mr. D "by two centuries, an elephant, and a lotus" – the meaning of which phrase Mr. D never quite understood.

At the other end of the room, we climb a coiling staircase that I'm told goes all the way up to the third floor, to the Spanish Room.

"A Moorish arabesque cabinet from the fifteenth-century Spanish Renaissance," as Mr. D explains, reigns in the midst of this room. The cabinet resembles Mr. D's secretaire, except this one has lots of drawers and doors that flip open, then close back as if they're alive.

"I bought this rare piece at an auction in London, in the eighteen hundreds," Mr. D says. He opens a secret door that has the Dragon sign on it. On the other side is the Music Room.

This chamber is bathed in a soft candlelight. Cobwebs and dust are everywhere. I reach the instruments: a piano missing its legs; a clavier with no keys, which the mice have turned into a shelter; a rusted harp with only two strings, hanging on a hook; a pear-shaped mandolin with three necks, one broken; a rusted flute with dozens of finger holes; an English horn big as an elephant tusk.

I approach the mandolin and brush my fingers over its strings. It puffs and begins to play a sad lied. The harp coughs and vibrates its last strings. Then the chimes join with their crystal-bells sound. From the floor, the piano plays a bass arpeggio for the left hand. Through five holes that have escaped rusting, the flute whistles somewhat out of tune. When the English horn blows a long powerful end note, it spreads all the dust from the room, which gathers into a cloud that floats below the ceiling, then falls and tears the cobwebs apart, scaring some spiders and a few moths. Upon gloriously wrapping up the song, all the instruments resume their still positions.

"Can you play something else?" I ask the mandolin.

"Sorry, it's been a long time. We used to play 'Peter and the Wolf.' But I forgot all the songs, and nobody knows where the scores are. Do you?"

"No, I'm not from around here. I'm just passing through, and – "

"Don't you know *any* songs?"

"Oh, but I do. I'm a soloist with the chorus of the Pointed-Hats Wizardry School."

"Then sing something and we'll accompany you."

"Who are you talking to?" Mr. D asks from a far corner of the room, where he's searching through some rusted organ pipes.

I strike a pose and sing the refrain of "The Little Witch Apprentice Song," which I have performed with great success for the end-of-term festivities:

> *There was a little witchy witch,*
> *A pretty little witch.*
> *They say she was never sad or bad,*
> *For she was always bright and glad.*
> *And her name was Mari-gold, Mari-gold*
> *Marigold of Salem!*

The instruments follow me up to a point when the piano delivers passionate variations on the theme, the flute chirps like a bird announcing rain, and the mandolin warbles high-pitched notes like a soprano. When the English horn releases a strong note resembling an elephant's call to battle, Mr. D jumps from behind the organ pipes.

"Enough!" he yells at the instruments. "Marigold, what if the castle guards heard you? I forgot to tell you – this is the Mad Orchestra."

"How dare you, sir?" the piano says.

"He's an ignorant," the harp says.

"Where's your musical education, mister?" the mandolin yells, snapping a string.

I try to bring peace. "I think there's been a misunderstanding here – "

"He has to apologize first!" the flute says.

"In any case, I'm not talking to him," the English horn says.

Mr. D takes his cloak in his hands and bows like an artist in front of his audience. "Ladies and gents, I deeply apologize for the blunder I've made. It's not my fault. It's the twentieth century's fault. Today people don't appreciate classical music as they used to, they'd rather watch movies. And television has gotten to me, too. I'm not immune to it, you know – "

"I told you he's an ignorant," the harp tells the piano.

"But I do know by heart Violetta Valery's aria from the opera 'La Traviata,'" Mr. D says.

"Let's hear it, mister," the mandolin says.

Mr. D starts singing "*Addio, del passato*" with a terribly coarse voice that's completely out of tune.

"Have pity!" the English horn yells at Mr. D. "You'll deafen us all."

But Mr. D sings on.

"Did you hear that?" Mr. D asks, stopping in mid-note.

A whoosh, then a woman's voice laments in the dark. Frightened, the instruments have turned quiet.

"Who's there?" Mr. D asks.

The voice keeps wailing.

"Come out where I can see you."

When the crying gets stronger, a bluish-white creature with big holes instead of eyes and a moon-shaped hollow for a mouth shows up through the wall.

A ghost!

Its silhouette changes as it swishes, passing through instruments, covering them with its ashy body.

"Help me," the ghost says. "I'll drown. Help me!"

"Hello to you, too." Mr. D looks surprised yet entertained by the apparition. "For one thing, at your present state you've already drowned."

"No!" The ghost bursts into a high-pitched cry. It covers its face with its smoky hands and flies to the opposite corner of the room.

"I'm sorry to bring you such news," Mr. D says. "Do you think I liked it when I was told I'd be undead for the rest of my life? No. But I got over it. In fact, I'm proud of it now. Think of it this way, nothing in the world can harm you now."

"But I'll drown," the ghost says between sobs.

"All right, let's start from the beginning," Mr. D says. "What's your name?"

"My name is Ileana, and I'm the most beautiful girl in the county."

"I can see that."

"Be nice to it," I tell Mr. D. "Don't you see it's collapsing?"

"I had wheat-blond braids and a white lace wedding dress," the ghost says, puffing up. "But now I'm just the ghost from the Princely Dormitory. I was sleeping, but the singing woke me up." It wipes away a few tears with the hem of its ashy gown's sleeve. "I was supposed to get married, but just before my wedding they killed our story."

"Your what?" I ask.

"Our story. They came and killed all the fairy tales, legends, and myths."

"Who's they?" I ask.

"Those creatures dressed in black. They threw our storybook in a river – that's when I drowned."

"Black Suits?" Mr. D asks.

"Yes," the ghost says. "They've started coming here lately."

"Those darned Black Suits," Mr. D says. "They'll pay, I promise you."

"That's not all," the ghost says. "Every time they destroy a book that has my story in it, they kill me again. It never ends."

"Listen," Mr. D tells the ghost, "I'm searching for a musical instrument. Maybe you've seen it around."

"What is it?"

"A small golden lyre I got from a seventeenth-century auction in Florence."

"I think I saw it, maybe half a century ago," the ghost says. "There, behind those violins. Isn't that what you're looking for?"

Mr. D jumps in the violin section. Hidden behind strings, he finds his magic lyre.

"I don't think you'll need me any more." The ghost vanishes into the Spanish Room with one last wail that it's going to drown.

It never said goodbye, and I feel sorry for it.

"This is an ancient magic device," Mr. D says, holding the lyre to his chest. He explains that once the lyre is plugged into the Vampire Organ from the Cathedral, it will activate a special wave connecting all the vampires in the country. "It's a special energy wave the Black Suits can't detect. But for now," he says, looking at his watch, "we need to hurry out of here -- "

Mr. D freezes, his ears stretched like a wolf's.

There's a commotion on the second floor. I recognize the voice of the castle guard Mr. D scared earlier. He's probably returning with at least three people.

"I'm telling you," he says, "it's Dracula. I swear it's him. Poor George, he was just joking when Dracula showed up. I told George to be more cautious – you never know who's listening."

Their steps sound closer. I'm frantic. We need an escape. Quick!

Just when the guards are about to open the door to the Music Room, the ghost shows up and covers us with its dress.

"Keep quiet," it says. "You're invisible inside my gown."

The door smashes open. Five castle guards storm in, ready to attack. Since they can't see us, they find only a place full of old broken rusted instruments. They stare and listen until they make sure nothing's moving or breathing in the room.

Just as they're about to leave, the ghost accidentally lets out a little wail – probably because it thinks it's going to drown.

Mr. D doesn't wait. He dashes from under the ghost's smoky dress and plunges his fangs into a castle guard's neck. The others freak out but don't leave their positions. I'm petrified.

Mr. D leaves two castle guards dead on the floor, while the others flee so quickly I swear they've grown an extra pair of legs. Satisfied, Mr. D wipes his fangs with a dragon-embroidered handkerchief, then rushes out of the room to chase the last guards.

Alone in the Music Room and still curious about the mandolin, I approach it to listen to its sad song once more. A noise behind the open door stops me. My stomach lurches.

Somebody leaps in my direction – it's the one-eyed castle guard who survived his first encounter with Mr. D.

He tries to catch me, but I flee through the room, hopping over instruments, throwing a trumpet, a flute, and a violin bow in his direction. Still, he's getting closer. I'm hoping Mr. D will come to my rescue. But he doesn't show up.

Quick! The magic Roma vials in my knapsack.

I duck behind the piano, frantically searching for one of them. The castle guard approaches – he's grinning as he thrusts his right hand to get me. Where are the vials? Where? My fingers grab hold of one. I raise it before my eyes to see that it's the green one-hour spell kind, then drop it on the floor and crush it with my right foot, wishing the castle guard were a toad.

The wretched man vanishes. In his place a greenish-brown bullfrog squats and croaks on the back of a broken violin. By the Salem witches' wands! What a powerful spell.

The frog squints at me and pumps up the balloons around its mouth. When Mr. D reappears in the room, it leaps into a tuba.

"What was that? Did I just hear a frog?"

"Yes," I say, "but only for an hour."

"What does that mean?'"

"I just turned a castle guard into a toad. But only for an hour."

Mr. D chuckles, saying he never thought I was such a powerful witch.

"No, it wasn't me," I say. "It was the spell vial I got from Zaraza."

"I see," Mr. D says. "Never mind, one day you'll become a great witch!"

I nod, tentatively. After all, I've never used witch magic. But in three years I'll show everybody who I really am – assuming I ever get out of this place alive.

I say goodbye to the instruments. When I get to the mandolin, it yells at me, "Teach him how to sing, will you?"

"Yeah, yeah," Mr. D says, scowling.

What a funny bunch!

We exit the Music Room through a different door. Upon finding the kitchen, Mr. D jumps in the garbage chute and drags me after him. As I glide on this roller coaster, I imagine I'm back in Luna Park, where I twisted my ankle last year.

But when I fall into the mine again, I realize I'm so far away from Salem, I may never see Luna Park again.

11. Maria Dracula

Mr. D's eyes again turn into a source of light. We walk in those pitch-black subterranean places until we reach a heavy fir door.

As we push the door open, a smell of dead rats overwhelms us. Phew!

"The castle's torture dungeons," Mr. D says with a grin, pointing at the dark cellars.

In a chamber to my right, a giant oblong iron device is left wide open. The strange contraption has hinges on one side and closes like a mummy's casket. But what's with all the rusted spikes?

"What is this?" I ask.

"It's the Iron Maiden," Mr. D says. "It belonged to Countess Elizabeth Bathory, a sixteenth-century Transcarpathian countess obsessed with eternal youth and beauty." The countess used the Iron Maiden to squeeze the blood of some six hundred maidens from the villages around. "She bathed in their blood, hoping she would stay forever young."

A shiver runs up my spine.

Mr. D closes the blood-squishing thing. A woman's mask shows up carved in metal on the front half. Her eyes and hands closed in prayer, she grins at me from behind long hairs. Her nasty smirk terrifies me.

"Did you ever meet her?" I ask Mr. D.

"I did. She was charming. Of course, I didn't know what she was really up to." He remembers being unable to guess her age. Countess Bathory, dressed up in a blue gown made entirely of lace, played the clavier and sang a lied. Her skin was very white, as if she were dead, and her lips incredibly red. "It shocked even me! She had a nice voice and I might have fallen in love with her, but I was still mourning Marga. Now she's been dead for centuries, and her body is buried in an unknown place, her soul lost forever."

What a terrible story! This Transcarpathian murderess was worse than the wicked witches from the Black Hollow Lake who stole people's souls. At least they didn't put them in horrible devices to squeeze their blood. Maybe this countess was a fake wicked witch who became so cruel because she couldn't use magic.

"What's in here?" I ask, reaching a chamber full of pikes.

"That's the reserve. But. . .I never used it," Mr. D says. "There's not much left after five centuries – aside from a bear trap, some whips, and a cage where I put the traitors. But it wasn't the cage that scared them most, it was the impaling."

By the Salem witches' wands! Mr. D is confessing, right here and now, that he *impaled* people.

"I just wanted to protect the country," he says. "Looking back, I may have been too harsh, like that time when I left a forest of head-impaled pikes." Mr. D explains that impaling was common in the Middle Ages. Spanish kings and German lords used it with great success. "I suppose I got famous too quickly with my pikes and all, but it's not my fault." The *Saxon Chronicles* publicized his deeds beyond any truth. "Anyway, we're in modern times now, and I've changed."

There's a noise coming from the walls around us. What can be on our tracks: gargoyles, castle guards, Black Suits? But none of these turns up. Instead a pack of fluttering bats emerges from dozens of holes in the walls. They smell terrible. They smell dead.

"These bats live below the mountain, in the caves," Mr. D says. "They used to show up and suck blood from my prisoners." He catches a bat by the wings, bites off its head, and eats it the way he did at the Theater of Vaudeville. Disgusting! Unable to look at his face, I turn away.

"Why did you do that?" I ask.

"Do what?"

"Why did you eat that bat's head?" A grayish bat flies in front of my face, peering at me with little crossed eyes.

Mr. D senses my upset and says in a mellow voice, "Marigold, I'm sorry. It's just that I was so hungry – I couldn't help myself." He throws away the doomed creature's leftover wings and claws. "Wouldn't you have done the same?"

"Never," I say, shooing away another bat. "Do you eat anything besides bats?"

"Honestly," Mr. D says, "I've changed my diet these days – I'm not on blood alone any more. There's some of that, but mostly I'm doing quite well on pasta and bread, fruits and veggies. I had to cut down on sugar, especially chocolate – if only you knew how much I loved it."

If only he knew there's someone else who loves chocolate even more.

"Also, I hate alcohol," Mr. D says. "Our vampire stomachs can't take it. The other thing we can't stand is smoking. It ruins our lungs, sense of smell, and taste. And we also stay away from garlic, which stinks and isn't good for us either. This is the twentieth century. Enough of the gothic stuff."

"But Mr. D, you ate a bat, and you just said you've changed." I take a bite from a wafer I took out of my knapsack.

"C'mon Marigold, don't make such a fuss about my eating habits. I do have to eat, you know. Let's just forget about it. I promise I'll try to do better."

With the bats fluttering around us like insects around a lightbulb, all of a sudden it strikes me hard.

"Mr. D, now that you've found your magic lyre, don't you think it's time to find my relative? " I say, staring at him boldly. "Besides, in a couple of hours it'll already be Thursday."

Mr. D closes his eyes as if he's meditating about some serious business. When he opens them again, he glances at his watch and says, "Of course, Marigold! It's time to keep my promise. Let's hurry, before the sun catches up with us."

My heart throbs at the thought that Mother-the-hurtling-star and I will finally meet our last ancestor. I wave goodbye to Castle Bran and its wondrous creatures and climb on Mr. D's lizard back.

We take the passage to the village at the foot of the mountain. The village seems to quietly glow, stars reflecting in windowpanes. A few cottages away from us, a watchdog barks and a confused rooster crows at the moon. Somebody throws a bucket of water at the rooster.

Mr. D and I tiptoe on the main street covered with gravel until we pass a fearsome pack of dogs. They bark furiously at Mr. D while I hang on tight to his body. We're sure to be chased.

I'm right! Mr. D leaps over the dogs' heads, and the hunt is on. The dogs are close enough to bite Mr. D's tail, but they miss his legs.

A few candles light up in the windows, showing astonished faces, hands making crosses in the air. A door opens and a kid yells, "*Draculea, draculea* is back! Watch out!"

For a while the dogs nip at our heels. Mr. D suddenly turns and roars at them, and they stop for a moment, then resume barking fiercely after us.

Alarmed by the noise, a few peasants wait for us at the other end of the village. They fetch river stones and fling them at us, hitting Mr. D in several places. He yells in pain but runs even faster, roaring and scaring the peasants back into their homes.

When at last we reach the forest, a pebble hits me in the head, opposite the knuckle left by the comet attack. It hurts so badly that I'm afraid I'm going to faint. With two little horns on my forehead, I'll surely look like a wicked witch.

Fearful that the peasants might still be in pursuit, Mr. D continues running through the dark woods.

"Slow down," I say.

Wheezing, he tells me the villagers have sour memories from their great-grandparents' time, when at night he'd prey on them, feasting off their blood.

"How can I ever get close enough to tell them I'm sorry? That's why I've changed, Marigold."

By the time a new knuckle grows on my forehead, we stop in a glade that shines eerily, like a lake of mercury. Bathed in moonlight, a small monastery made of glass rises in its midst. The door is wide open. Inside, a witch spins a glowing thread on a wheel.

I can't guess the witch's age, but she's so creased she looks centuries old. She doesn't resemble the witches back home: She looks like nature, with her long gown of burgundy leaves, her slippers of bark, her green hair of moss.

"Who is she, Mr. D?"

"She's a forest witch. You see them only once in a lifetime."

"What's she doing?"

"She's spinning the Thread of Time on the Time Wheel." Mr. D explains it's the witch's responsibility to keep time flowing at a certain pace – not too slow, not too fast – just as all humans and creatures should live according to the Laws of Time. "Even I have to abide by these laws. Marga wanted to change them so her life as the undead would pass quicker. But the Laws of Time told Marga that was forbidden."

"Why?" I ask, recalling my voyages through the Time Gates.

"You see, the Laws of Time are connected to the Laws of the Universe," Mr. D says. "If time changed, everything in the universe would change." He says that is why it is forbidden to modify the length of seconds, minutes, hours, days, months, and years – for then the entire world would change.

"Then the Magic Corridors through space and time . . ." I whisper.

"Yes, they are the Laws of the Universe," Mr. D says. "But I haven't gone through the space corridors yet. Nobody knows where they are. Maybe you do?"

"No, Mr. D. Really, I don't recall how I ended up on Bookrest's streets. You know, the comet hit me and then – "

"Beloved," the witch says just as we're about to leave the glade.

"What?" Mr. D says.

"Beloved," the witch says again, "do you still have the rosebud?"

"What rosebud? Who are you?"

"The red rosebud I gave you, beloved."

"I do have a red rosebud, but I don't recall your giving it to me. My dearest Marga, my true love, gave it to me back in . . . "

I stop breathing, and so does Mr. D.

"Marga?" he asks, his voice trembling.

"Beloved, do you still have my letter?"

Mr. D falls to his knees. "What kind of trick is this?"

"No trick, beloved. You just have to remember."

"Remember what?"

"Remember me and what made me so unhappy that I wanted – I needed – to leave."

Mr. D is quiet for a moment, then says, "Time is what upset you. Eternity. The fact that you were never going to die."

"Yes, beloved. I hated living as a vampire, as the undead."

"But what about me?" Mr. D asks Marga-the-witch in this improvised moonlit confessional.

"Beloved, I knew you'd be fine." The witch moans, then she says, "I knew you'd understand that it takes more than a vampire body to be a vampire and live forever. I couldn't do it, but I've always loved you and always will."

"What happened to you?" Mr. D asks.

"I ran into the forests until I found the dying forest witch. She was a thousand years old and couldn't spin the wheel

132

any longer, so time began flowing slower than usual." Marga-the-witch tells him that the day had grown to thirty hours and the night forty hours long. All the animals in the forest slept during daytime and people in the village stopped working. Crops died, rivers flooded, and the sun chased the moon, ready to burn it out of the sky. Seeing her so unhappy, the forest witch suggested Marga become the new forest witch and live for another nine hundred years.

"Forest witches live for a thousand years. So, having already lived for a century, I took the offer – and now I'm four centuries short of dying. Isn't that wonderful?"

Mr. D sobs agate-red tears that splash in the grass, leaving rusty spots.

I get a bit of courage and ask Marga-the-witch, "And what happened to the witch before you?"

"She died, and her body became part of the trees and flowers of this forest. She may even be listening now." She tells me that like all forests, this one is alive. But today all the spirits, fairies, and witches have withdrawn into the depths of the earth. She blames the Black Suits who've recently started trespassing into Transcarpathia and preying on the forests. "Somebody has to stop them."

"Can't you do anything about it?" I ask. "With the Time Wheel, I mean?"

"Time is sacred. Besides, if I delayed time, the Black Suits would live longer. And if I rushed time, I'd kill all souls – human and animal – in just one day."

With that, she spins her wheel, which makes her glass monastery take off like a shuttle. They disappear in the moonlight, leaving something shiny in the dew-wet grass.

Mr. D crawls toward the object and takes it in his hands. He stares at it and sobs like a child. Caressing it, he says, "This is Marga's medallion. It's the last thing I ever gave her." Apparently, the golden medallion hides a lock of her hair. "Here, you take it," he says, handing me the medallion. "I'm giving it to you. It'll protect you whenever you're in danger."

Its soft polished surface has letters engraved on it: M. D. Marga Dracula.

I open the medallion and take out a black lock of hair. It smells like sweet fennel. Behind the hair I find a small portrait –

Marga's. I stare into her deep-set eyes. Strangely, they're gazing back at me from centuries beyond.

Mr. D rests in silence, head down, eyes closed, his giant hands covering his heart.

I drop on the grass near him and listen to the crickets. The forest witch may be listening to us. And what about Marga? She turned out to be a witch – but a good one and mortal, like all witches. Would I ever agree to trade my mortality as a witch for a vampire's eternal life? No, I don't think so. There would be no way back unless I found another forest witch – like Marga did – and exchanged my eternity for her thousand-years life.

I doze for a while. When I awaken, a falling star hurtles across the sky. Maybe it's Mother searching for me on the ground. I wave – although I know she can't respond. Still, I follow the star as it vanishes behind the moon.

Mr. D's face looks white and wrinkled, like crumpled paper, so ancient that only now do I fully believe that I've been in the company of a five-century-old creature.

"Arghhh!" he screams.

Sprawled, Mr. D jerks as if he's been struck by lightning. His eyes have turned white. Foam flecks his mouth. He's clearly in pain.

"Mr. D, what's wrong?"

"It's from my latest encounters with the Black Suits," he cries. "I don't think Zaraza's spells work any more." He writhes on the grass.

Poor Mr. D, the Black Suits have drained him.

"Listen here, Marigold. I meant to tell you this for some time now." He tries to strand up, but cringes and falls back, wailing. "Besides, I have to keep my promise."

From a secret pocket hidden in the red linen of his cloak, Mr. D pulls out what appear to be two letters.

"Here, take these."

The first one is an etching in black ink, the portrait of a little girl with dark hair and melancholy eyes. I look more carefully. It's me! But the name under the portrait reads: Maria Dracula.

"What is this?" I ask Mr. D.

His hands trembling, Mr. D keeps silent. Finally he says with a serious voice, "Marigold, I think it's finally time for you to know who you really are."

"Who is this?" I ask, pointing at the etching. "And why does she look like me?"

"It *is* you." Mr. D says, his fangs wobbling over his lower lip.

"But how did you get this? And who drew it? I mean, how could anyone draw me if we never met before?"

"I asked the Roma painters to make it using one of Marga's portraits, from when she was a little girl. I always figured you must look like her."

"Wait a minute! Why would I look like Marga?"

"Because your real Transcarpathian name is Maria Dracula."

What trick is this?

"Excuse me, what does it mean my real name is Maria Dracula?" I'm staring at Mr. D as if he's crazy. Or am I?

Mr. D sighs and gives me a tender look. "It means you're my long-sought great-granddaughter."

By the Salem witches' wands! Okay, say my ancestors may have come from Transcarpathia, but what sane person would ever believe she's Dracula's descendant?

"Your mother," Mr. D says, "is my granddaughter. You come from a long line of respected Salem witches on your grandmother's side and vampire princes on mine. Now that I know you, I'm sure of it – you're my flesh and blood. And you've got Marga's eyes."

"Then . . .are *you* my last ancestor from Transcarpathia?"

Mr. D doesn't say anything, but his glinting eyes answer my question. Now I get it. During my time here I've had to prove myself worthy of my heritage, and only now am I being recognized as a Dracula.

"How did all this happen?"

"It all goes back to Lydia, our daughter," Mr. D says.

"You had a daughter?"

"Yes, but she never became a vampire." Mr. D explains that Lydia left for the New World in the 1600's. She wrote back a couple of times, saying she'd settled in the village of Salem and studied the native Indians' healing ways in order to cure the children struck with smallpox.

In another letter Lydia confessed that she'd found unusual powers through her experiments with local herbs. Although she couldn't have an afterlife like a vampire, she could still live for a few good centuries. She could fly at night and cast spells, talk to cats and use magic wands, and she called herself a herbs witch.

"I've kept one of Lydia's letters," Mr. D says. "Open the other one," he whispers.

The ancient stained piece of paper with calligraphic letters reads:

November 4, 1692
Village of Salem

Dear Father,
This day, one hundred and thirty two years since my birth, I find myself accused of black witchcraft. I do not have the time to tell you how wrong this is. I have always wanted to help my fellow people in the village and heal their ailments. My friends, Sarah Morey and Susannah Martin, have already been hanged.
I have to abandon Salem, to save my newborn baby girl. I will leave with her father, Ocean-Wave-By-Night, and his Massachuset tribe band. I hope you'll hear from me again, maybe in the next century.

Your daughter,
Lydia Dracula

"The newborn baby girl was your mother, Dorothy. She was Lydia's daughter and my granddaughter," Mr. D says, his eyes sad. This is who he was expecting to arrive from Salem. But Mr. D never knew he also had a great-granddaughter. He thought that Dorothy, being the last herbs witch of Salem, was Maria Dracula. "But it's you!"

My heart pounding, I stare at Mr. D, trying to find some resemblance to Mother, then to me. But no, there's nothing in that gargoyle face to suggest any similarity – except perhaps for the kindness I sometimes read in his eyes.

But Mr. D's revelation about my ancestry makes me stronger in an unexpected way. After all, I'm a herbs witch from a long-line of witches and vampires!

When the moon's half-coin face spreads its light over the dew-wet grass, Mr. D tells me that Lydia died in the late 1800's, by which time she'd lived with the Massachuset tribe band in the north, in the Dominion of Canada.

"But when her husband died, after the 1776 War of Independence, she moved back to Salem and resumed living in the same house, in the Twisted-Wand District."

Mr. D is talking about the ivy-wrapped cottage with an attic full of pointed witch hats and herbs recipes where Mother and I grew up. But one aspect of being Dracula's descendant is troubling me.

"Mr. D, if I'm a witch on Mother's side but a Dracula on your side, does that make me a vampire?"

"No, you're only a little Salem herbs witch."

"How can you be sure?"

"Because Lydia was born before Marga and I became vampires," Mr. D says. "Vampire blood never flowed in Lydia's or Dorothy's veins – although they did become witches. But you're still a Dracula princess, and that's why the Dracula Treatise applies to you."

I stare at him, entranced.

"And by now I know that my brave descendant is you, Marigold of Salem. You are Maria Dracula."

I call my new name a couple of time to get used to it. Again I stare at the etching, then set it down, where the clover surrounds it like a natural green frame.

I'm still reeling from everything that's happened to me these past few days. I recall Zaraza's firefly taking refuge in my kaleidoscope, Waltz plunging into the Sapphire Sea, the Oracle-willow keeping me hostage in the City of Whispers, the Sapphire Sea Dragon dropping gems to be melted into the sea, Red kissing me in the train. I'll surely miss everyone and everything from this faraway place!

Mr. D says he feels unusually weak. He wheezes, like he's going to expire.

We're at the border of the Enchanted Forest. Mr. D calls the Romas, asking them to carry him back to Castle Bran, "where Mr. Shadow will take care of me. But you," he says, pointing at me, "you'll have to make it back to Bookrest on your own." He howls as if he were on his deathbed, then says, "And since you are Maria Dracula, you'll have to take my place."

"Excuse me?" The stars begin circling around my head.

"You have to lead the V-kids' army into the fight against the Black Suits," Mr. D says, leaving me as numb as that time when the comet got me.

In my present frame of mind I'm not sure whether I'm happy to know I'm Dracula's long-sought great-granddaughter or not.

"And what if I can't make it?" I ask, hoping I sound like a shy little girl who's exempt from doing anything too difficult until she reaches witch age.

"You *will* make it!" Mr. D says. "Trust your Dracula instincts. They've served you well until now, don't you think?" He winks a fluttering eyelid.

"But Mr. D – "

"Oh, and take this." He hands over the magic lyre. "Don't forget to give it to the V-kids. They'll know what to do with it." Fangs out, eyes rolling, Mr. D shivers once more. Then he suddenly goes stiff as a stick.

Is he dead-undead? By the Salem witches' wands! How can Mr. D do this to me?

Even after the Romas hoist Mr. D in a wagon and head in a procession for Castle Bran, deep down in my heart I still cherish a little hope that Mr. D will somehow stand up again, like nothing has happened.

Then he'll lead the army and the fight, like the great vampire he is. And I won't have to do anything special, and all of this will have proved to be just a figment of my tired imagination.

12. The Battle in Sadness Square

How can Mr. D do this to me?

On my way back to Bookrest, I stand mute and angry like a wicked witch, lying on a rug carpet spread on the floor of a Roma canopy wagon. By the Salem witches' wands! I should never have put foot in Bookrest.

Back at the Cathedral, little Rose holds hands with Mrs. Snippety Smith.

"Marigold," Mrs. Snippety Smith says, gently pushing Rose forward, "may I present you my adopted daughter?"

Rose holds a drawing of a thistle above which she has written, "My New Mother."

I'm happy for Mrs. Snippety Smith and little Rose but saddened at the thought that with Mr. D sick, I've again ended up alone.

"Hello, everybody! I'm here, alive and well. What? You thought you'd get rid of me so easily?" It's Red, emerging from the eastern tunnel. He looks at me with his forever fall-in-love-with-me-Marigold smile.

The V-kids, who haven't noticed my blushing, assault Red with questions. "Zelda said you found your mother." "How is she?" "Is she nice?" "Does she love you?" And "Where is she now?"

"She's fine, very nice, yes she does, and when I told her about the Underground we both thought it was best for her to stay by the Sapphire Sea," Red says. "Losing her once was enough."

"How about the fight at the museum? How did you escape?" the V-kids ask.

And now I know what Red likes most – to boast about how brave a vampire he is. "So when three Black Suits jumped me, I tossed Apollo's oracle into their wicked faces." But the enemy kept chasing him among sarcophagi and statues, amphorae and spears – which he'd occasionally fling back, smashing the Black Suits' heads but crushing the precious historical vestiges "into a gazillion pieces. Then I shot them with Roma magic ink until they fried and melted to the last bone." He's sorry about the devastation of the museum, "but there was nothing else I could do to get out alive."

"How did you get separated from your mother originally?" Mrs. Snippety Smith asks.

"She lost me to the Black Suits ten years ago, on Baby Theft Night," Red says. During that night the Black Suits broke into as many homes as they could and stole all the babies they found. They attacked the parents who defended their children, even killed them if they resisted. "They got into my home" – Red's voice is deep, low, and sad – "and before they snatched me, they killed my father."

We grow perfectly still at this part of the gruesome story. A V-kid whispers that this is what must have happened to his family too.

"Was your mother afraid – I mean, that you're a v-vampire?" Rose says.

"No. She heard something about orphans who were saved and turned into vampires, but until she met me she thought it was just a rumor. She doesn't care if I'm a vampire – she says I'll always be her son. And if we defeat the Black Suits for good, I want to relocate by the Sapphire Sea and live with Mother."

There you have it! He's going away. Never mind me.

"Marigold, how are you?" Red asks, walking up as if he has just noticed me. "Did you ever get to Transcarpathia?"

I want to tell him all about the Mad Orchestra and the wailing ghost, the Bears' Cave and the Iron Maiden. But why should I?

"There," I say with a flat voice, handing him the magic lyre. "Take this. Mr. D said you know what to do with it – "

"But where *is* Mr. D?" Red says as he sends his jacket to the dry-cleaning on a flying hanger.

"Sick!"

"What do you mean, sick?" He drops onto a chair carved with wolves.

I him about Marga-the-witch and how the heartbroken Mr. D fell prey to a sudden weakness.

"The Romas took him back to Castle Bran."

"Oh, no! Who's going to lead the battle now?" Red asks.

"I am."

"What?"

"That's what Mr. D said"

"But you're just a girl!" Red says.

"So what? You think you're better just because you have fangs?" I look down and Meow nods, tentatively.

"That's not what I meant," Red says. "But you said you're not a witch. And, well . . .do you even know how to fight?"

"Ask the Midgets who helped them scare away the Black Suits drilling in the Cathedrals' ceiling," I say.

The Midgets nod toward me, then at Red. I turn to the Hawks.

"Who helped you rescue Mr. D at the orphanage?"

The Hawks nod at me, then at Red.

"Not to mention saving *your* life, or maybe you -- "

"All right, all right," Red says. "But Marigold, don't you think I should lead the battle? I *am* Mr. D's assistant."

"I know." I brace my arms, looking above the V-kids' heads like I'm the queen of witches. "But for your information, my true name is Maria Dracula."

Red's face lights up with wonder. He hollers, calling all the V-kids from the Cathedral.

"She's Maria Dracula, Maria Dracula . . . " The vampire children's voices echo in the grotto with lightning speed.

"So, it's you!" Red's eyes are glowing, his voice is vibrant.

"Excuse me?"

"Maria Dracula, it's *you!*" Red explains that ever since Mr. D took him as his assistant, he talked about a relative of his lost somewhere in the world, "a granddaughter or something, and he'd always hoped to reunite with her." They waited, year after year, but since nobody showed up, Red eventually decided Mr. D was imagining things.

Red looks at me as if he sees me for the first time. "Told you you're pretty, didn't I?"

I blush, again, and Red kisses me. Again. Where's Waltz to throw me that unmistakable look?

"And how should I call you now?" Red asks. "Marigold of Salem or Maria Dracula?"

I raise my shoulders, then let them drop. "Maybe Marigold. Nobody's ever called me by the other one," I say, afraid of what my new name brings with it.

"Maria Dracula, Maria Dracula . . ." The V-kids are still saying.

"You're right!" Red says. "You're going to lead the battle."

If only I could take my words back, but now it's too late. By the Salem witches' wands! Like it or not, I am Maria Dracula.

But I don't know how to be her. And I sure don't know how I'm going to lead an army of vampire children into battle.

Red grabs the lyre. Surrounded by a few Midgets and Hawks, we jump behind the Vampire Organ and stumble upon the sleeping Golem. Waltz naps in the giant's lap.

"Waltzie," Red says, "where have you been, boy?"

"Where haven't I?" Waltz woofs, morose yet happy to have found Red again. Zelda sent him back to Bookrest, after the pirates and I went off to rescue Mr. D from the Time Gate.

Red's eyes brighten at the news of our adventures throughout the Sapphire Sea. Waltz continues his story, while Red climbs the Golem – up to his shoulders, then high on his head, where he reaches the Vampire Organ's topmost pipe. He drops the magic lyre inside. There's a click, then the organ seems to come to life.

We take a few strides back and Red jumps in the Golem's lap.

The organ's pipes release a choking smoke, which slowly turns to whitish vapor. Each pipe begins to play a special note – from the highest pitched, whose sound cracks a few glasses, to the lowest, which makes the Cathedral shake like it's experiencing an earthquake.

The keyboard begins to play by itself a mysterious song resembling a polka. The pipes emit a strange wave that seems to catch all the V-kids by the ears. They sink to the ground and howl with pain, covering their ears.

"Stop it!" Red yells at me, jerking on the ground. "It'll kill us."

What should I do? I jump on the giant keyboard and leap from one key onto the next, hoping to play "Spring Ode to Salem."

I leap all over the keys until the organ stops its vampire-killer song and erupts in black vapors and ash. It stands still, puffing. When it resumes, the scary song energizes the V-kids, who jump to their feet with curious faces and chattering fangs.

"It's the vampire wave!" Red yells, calling the V-kids around the organ. "Listen!"

I can't hear a thing, and why should I? I'm not a vampire, I'm a Salem witch. Thank God for that!

But the vampire children gather around the Vampire Organ. Eyes closed, fangs pointing out, they listen to the polka in a trance.

The clock on the western wall sounds its eleventh gong, startling the V-kids. They awaken from whatever Vampire Organ magic got hold of them.

Red jumps on a boulder in the midst of the crowd and freezes into a glorious pose. His face opens into a big fanged smile and he raises his hands to the ceiling as if in an incantation.

"You've heard what the organ said. It's time to bring the Black Suits down!" Now howls like a wolf, imitating Mr. D. "And I believe we have a leader now –"

Oh, no! Here it comes –

"Marigold of Salem a. k. a. Maria Dracula!" Red announces and the grotto reverberates my name.

The V-kids hurry to dress in their spell-protected gear, bearing Dracula's Dragon on their plates and helmets.

"Take it -- your gear." Red hands me a pile of shiny metal. "If it doesn't fit, we can always trim or enlarge it with Roma spells."

I put on the formidable armor over Meow, hoping it's danger-proof. But just to make sure I have extra protection, I hang Marga's medallion around my neck and shove the red spell vial in my left pocket, glancing dolefully at my torn jeans.

Waltz prances around, dressed in an outfit that looks like a pipe, from which his legs, head, and tail jut out like they're attached to it.

Red and I cover our smirks – especially me, because after our teasing on the Sapphire Sea trip, I don't want to hurt the poodle's feelings again. But seeing Waltz's comical appearance, the V-kids laugh, their cackles resonating throughout the Cathedral.

Waltz yelps, obviously insulted, and runs away. I chase him and find him hiding behind the Golem.

"They're just kids," I tell him. "They don't know you're a brave poodle with an amazing command of other creatures' languages. We need you, Waltz – the Underground needs you."

With tears in his eyes, Waltz gives me his right paw, licks my left shoe, and purrs. I'm glad we're friends again. Then, tail up, he makes a proud return, woofing at the V-kids, "If you don't like it, don't look!"

By now all the V-kids are dressed in shiny warrior gear. They gather around and stare at me in silence, their vampire fangs sticking out.

"When are we going to attack?" Red asks.

Attack? I'm trying to put together a coherent sentence about excusing myself because my gear needs some magic trimming when something pushes me from behind – and somehow what comes out of my mouth is an ill-fated yet clear order: "Attack!"

Panic overwhelms me, but it's already too late to take my word back without looking goofy and scared – everything the army captain I'm expected to be is not.

But upon hearing my "Attack!" call reverberating throughout the Cathedral, all the V-kids have exploded, shouting that they're ready to fight the Black Suits, avenge their parents, and get even for their torment in the orphanage.

I don't budge from my spot, uncertain about what's going to happen next. The vampire children gather in three-file configurations, each with twelve kids. I count a total of eighteen files, which means two hundred and sixteen kids. But these are no ordinary kids – they're V-kids!

I lose my last excuse. The V-kids, seeing me all dressed up in my gear and with my helmet fitting despairingly well, ask me to lead them out.

The panic makes me choke inside that guerrilla armor, and I want to throw it away. But the V-kids don't give me a chance. They force me ahead of their army, barely leaving me time to call Red, the Golem, and Mrs. Snippety Smith.

Like a torrent of water released from a dam, the V-kids and I their anything-but-fearless leader pour out of the Cathedral and through the tunnels. These must for sure be the last hours of my life.

We reach the first sewer and climb up into the sunlight.

The V-kids holler out a pep song:

Ole, ole, ole, ole!
We're the V-kids with no parents.

Ole, ole, ole, ole!
We'll eat the Black Bug in two seconds.
Ole, ole, ole, ole!

We're out in Thriller Books Square. A sky wrinkled around a mustard-yellow sun has me feeling scorched like a scarab on fire.

My right palm tickles. My green herbs-witch line shines so bright I'm afraid it's going to burn my hand all the way through to the other side. But if this is a sign, then everything that's witchcraft inside of me could now awaken and help me prove to the V-kids – and to myself – that I'm a reliable Salem witch apprentice.

"So, what's the plan?" I ask Red.

He tunes his vampire ears' pavilions in the air – no doubt to listen to the vampire wave emitted by the organ – and says, "We have to seize the Black Castle."

But is there a backup plan? After meeting so many magical people and creatures in my voyages through Rondelia, it's sad not to have Mr. D or Zelda with me, the pirates or Zaraza, Marga-the-forest-witch or the ghost, the Sapphire Sea Dragon or even the Mad Orchestra. I feel alone. How did I end up just with children and a dog – okay, vampire children and a brave talking dog?

Mrs. Snippety Smith approaches – how could I have forgotten that I have a powerful Salem witch with me?

"Scared, are you?" Mrs. Snippety Smith says, looking big like a caribou and scary in her armor.

I try to mumble something.

"Marigold, who'd have thought that of all the witches of Salem you would lead an army of vampire children to battle in a foreign country?" She says this with a grin, slightly teasing but not malicious. "And you're not even a warrior witch."

"I know!"

"Are you ready to fight, then?"

Silent, I stare at my stained shoes. Chrysanthemum Crown's ugly grin pops up in my mind, then I hear my class yelling after me, "nerd witch, nerd witch, nerd witch. . ."

"Listen here," Mrs. Snippety Smith says, unexpected warmth woven into her voice, "you do what you can – just try your best. And never doubt yourself." She points to the Golem, who stands behind me. "We'll be here too, don't forget."

I search in the Golem's eyes, wishing he had a mouth to tell me what he thinks. The giant stares back at me, his humid little black eyes full of courage.

Suddenly I feel stronger. I have the force of the Golem with me, and the powerful arm of Mrs. Snippety Smith, and I have Red the brave V-kid, and Waltz the little poodle expert on foreign dialects. And behind me I've got an entire army of vampire kids. On top of which I'm not only a witch apprentice from Salem -- I'm also Dracula's great-granddaughter!

Who said I'm alone?

A few V-kids stand transfixed, listening in the air. They jot down some words on a yellow piece of paper, which they hand over to Red.

"News?" I ask Red.

"A message from the Cathedral. A few Midgets have stayed down there to centralize the news from the Vampire Organ and send them to our army."

With my heart pounding, I read the message:

Marigold,
Stay where you are.
The people of Bookrest will join you soon.
Long live the Underground,
Rose & the Midgets

Dressed in red – they say it's the color of revenge – the men and women of Bookrest join our V-kids army. Clubs and slings in their hands, pebbles in their pockets, they sing warrior songs of olden times, vowing to avenge their children and end their oppression at the hands of the Black Suits.

The afternoon sun is blazing, and the air feels wild. Thousands of voices resonate throughout the streets.

I listen to the army's buzz. They talk about freedom and death. A few humans ask the V-kids about their families, hoping to find a lost child. Again the reality that I'm this brave group's captain both terrifies and mystifies me – it's beyond my wildest imagination, and there's no turning back.

"News bulletin!" Red says, breaking my meditation, handing me another yellow piece of paper.

Marigold,
Move to Sadness Square.
Prepare for battle. Black Suits ambush ahead.
Long live the Underground,
Rose & the Midgets

"Do you know where Sadness Square is?" I ask Red.

"Four blocks away. That's where the Black Palace is."

This, then, is the decisive moment. "Red, Waltz, will you lead the way, please?"

"All right, smart girl," Waltz woofs, while Red nods like a general.

I ask Mrs. Snippety Smith to raise her arms and make the call. When she yells in her booming alto voice, "Troops, be ready – we're moving ahead!" even I feel mobilized.

We're on our way: Red and Waltz ahead, then I, followed by the Golem to my left and Mrs. Snippety Smith to my right, after which the V-kids and the people of Bookrest march, shouting and singing – one giant heart.

Just before we reach Sadness Square, Simon-Sea-Phantom and his band show up – loaded to their teeth with knives and stinking of Sapphire-Sea fish.

My trip to this faraway land has not been in vain. Not only have I discovered my true Dracula heritage, I've also found so many friends that now we are quite a band fighting together. And I, Marigold, the last herbs witch of Salem, am leading the battle!

The barricade of Black Suits – hundreds, probably – waits for us. They're dressed in black stretch suits that cover their heads like masks and make them resemble giant moths. Their bayonets are pointed at us. They ooze their acrid smell, which reaches us even a block away.

Beyond the barricade, the Black Palace shines eerily in the sunlight. The gloomy building barely resembles a castle. It has one oval pointed tower and, oddly, no windows. It seems to be made of a black metal that strikes me as more appropriate for a submarine or a locomotive than a princely dwelling.

We stop a hundred feet away from the Black Suits – my army and theirs glaring at each other. They look astonished that so many people and creatures have gathered against them. But where is the Black Bug leader?

The Black Suits send a hundred fighters against us. They approach like a black wave of mud, oil, and melted coal, and I decide the moment has come. I yell from the bottom of my lungs the only word I know that works.

"ATTACK!"

Like a red and golden tide, the humans and the V-kids dash around me. Red, Waltz, Mrs. Snippety Smith, and the Golem follow my command and lead them into the enemy.

With Red ahead, the V-kids jump on the Black Suits and staple their necks, sucking their blood. Then humans and pirates join the fray with their clubs and knives. Waltz bites legs.

Mrs. Snippety Smith plucks bayonets from hands and flings them away like useless sticks, then slaps and beats Black Suits barehanded, yelling, "Take that for stealing kids from their families!" She kicks a Black Suit's butt and slaps a few others. "You should never anger a Salem warrior witch trained in martial arts, sword, and spear." She leaves her victims knocked out on the pavement and forces her way through lines of panicked Black Suits, who flee at her approach.

Beams glowing from his star, the Golem fries the enemy to ash. He lifts two Black Suits at a time and throws them away like garbage. Others he pummels to the ground and hammers through the pavement as if they were nails.

Our blizzard-style attack takes the Black Suits by surprise, but soon reinforcements begin to shoot at us. In response, the V-kids join hands and whirl like a live wheel, quicker and quicker. They roll on the pavement and – full speed – catapult themselves into the snipers, smashing against them like a boulder. And the Black Suits fall, seven at a time.

When the night sends its veiled emissary clouds to see what horrors the battle has wrought on both sides, Red and I count a dozen wounded V-kids, but many more dead Black Suits.

All of a sudden, as if responding to a secret order, the Black Suits regroup and retreat into a compact black mass.

"I'd say this is a sign that we too should rest and regain forces," Red says.

Sweaty and dusty, I take off my armor and check on Meow. I can't find her on my chest, or around my waist, or in one of the T-shirt's sleeves, or on my back. But something moves inside my jeans' left pocket. I shove my hand in, and behind the red spell vial the cat is purring. She must have gotten so scared that she tore the hem of the T-shirt with her teeth and claws and took refuge in the pocket. Now she's just a painted cat who can glide around my clothes and under my gear like a lost feather.

"Don't worry," I tell her, "I'll sew you again on the shirt when we get back to Salem."

It's midnight in Sadness Square. Mother-the-falling-star hurtles five times across the sky, checking for me. I wave at her, hoping she saw me dressed up in my glittery armor, leading an entire army.

Groups of humans and V-kids are scattered around, dozing. We've just had supper – sandwiches filled with a brown mushroom paste the Fortune sisters whipped up in their magical kitchen. Mrs. Snippety Smith attends to the V-kids' wounds. The Golem clears the battlefield of Black Suits corpses, and the pirates tell goodnight stories from the far lands of Hindustania.

A shadow sneaks on a wall, freezing and arching, glancing down.

Is it possible it's Mr. Shadow? When did he show up from Transcarpathia? And what about Mr. D?

The shadow strangles a Black Suit, who cowers and falls. Two Black Suits jump to his aid. Mr. Shadow chokes them both, one with each long, pointed-fingernails hand. That done, it stretches and grows so big that it covers the entire wall. After which it diminishes to the size of a human shadow. It lurches toward me, and upon reaching my spot, coils on my shadow like a protective shield.

Suddenly there's a swooshing. The cherry trees that were lined up in the street are alive now, gathering around us.

They bow toward us, losing a few translucent flowers in the moonlight.

"What magic is this?" I ask Red.

"Roma witchcraft," he whispers. "Only the Romas can bring the inanimate to life, giving them souls."

By the Salem witches' wands! Back home we're forbidden to turn lifeless things into creatures.

The streetlamps flicker their lights, their shafts twirling like ribbons. They circle us, as do the blocks, whose tall buildings undulate like serpents.

I make out that they've joined our army.

Glad we're getting so big, I fall asleep in the Golem's lap, dreaming that I'm back in Salem, where I don't have to fight with anything until I reach witch age.

By the time the sun chases the night's veils out of the sky, we're already deep into the next day's fight. The tall buildings shake, stoop, and from a few unfinished stories fling scarlet bricks into a Black-Suits blockade of two hundred men. With their lights, the live streetlamps blind our enemies, and with their branches, the cherries bash Black Suits' heads.

The V-kids jump on the Black Suits to bite them, followed by pirates and other humans, who finish them off. Mrs. Snippety Smith is not quite as mighty a warrior today – she's beginning to flag – but she can still take out one Black Suit at a time. The Golem is as heroic as ever: he scoops up the Black Suits, breaks their necks and tosses them onto a growing pile of corpses.

Red and I lead the attack of the vampire-kids' wheels on the snipers.

At noon there's a commotion. Like waves, Black Suits jump over and over again, attacking the Golem. The giant fights, but I notice something strange in the way he keeps his left fist high above his head, fighting with the rest of his body.

Since Mrs. Snippety Smith and the pirates are busy on the front line, I set up a diversion – I send word throughout the army to yell, "Victory, victory!"

The kids are excited and keep biting necks and sucking blood, yelling that we've won.

The Black Suits' siege of the Golem comes to a halt. They regroup and listen. They leave the Golem and jump on the V-kids, only to be chased by humans and pirates, blasted by Mrs. Snippety Smith's unforgiving arm, and bitten by Red, who staples necks and leaps from shoulder to shoulder as if he has wings.

The Golem stands frozen, his knees, wrists, shoulders, elbows, and neck cracking. A dozen holes pierce his patched clothes and clay skin, as if an army of rodents has gnawed him. In his fist, above our heads, the Golem holds something that moves.

The Golem blinks at me twice, his friendly eyes filled with tears.

How is this possible? The Steins said the giant doesn't have a mind of his own.

From his umbrella-wide palm the Golem puts on the ground a trembling little boy. He has no fangs, he's human. Seeing that we're not Black Suits, the kid stops shaking. He gets a bit of courage and tells us the giant saved his life.

He had just escaped from an orphanage and wanted to join the army. He was running away from the orphanage guards when he reached the fight. Thinking the Golem was a gigantic toy, the boy climbed all the way up and hid in his giant's left hand, behind his huge fingers. The Golem closed his fist on the boy and whoever tried to snatch him – orphanage guards or Black Suits – would meet the Golem's rage. The giant wouldn't let go of the boy, no matter how many enemies jumped on him, no matter what they did to him: shooting, burning, spiking.

For the first time I realize that although the Golem and some other creatures in the world may not have minds of their own like humans do, this doesn't mean they don't have a heart. And I should never take for granted even the smallest pebble lying in the dusty road. Who knows? It too might have a soul.

"Red!" I shout, eager to tell him about the boy.
No answer.
"Red, where are you?" I turn, rush around. He's gone. "Red!"
Nothing.

Waltz emerges from the mass of fighting bodies. He runs toward me, yelping.

"Waltz, what's wrong?"

"It's Red. I think he – "

Under a rain of black arrows, I dash away behind wheels of V-kids and finally reach Red behind a cherry tree. He lies sprawled on the pavement, blood trickling from his chest, his arms and legs spread out, his face stiff and white, his eyes closed.

I feel numb, horrified. What can I do? I remember the red spell vial I got from Zaraza. Who cares if I'm not going to use it for a deadly twenty-four-hour magic? I need it now, and it had better work! With trembling fingers I take the ampoule out of my jeans' left pocket, where Meow has kept it safe and warm.

Carefully I drip the bubbling liquid on Red's chest. Nothing. He lies there rigid like a corpse.

"Red! Please, wake up!"

A few tears have washed my face and fallen onto Red's chest. Mixed with Zaraza's spell and Red's blood, they create a simmering reaction. Red's eyelids are still closed, but now they flutter in distress. He's alive!

"Hurry!" I say, calling two Hawks. I tell them to take Red down to the Cathedral.

But they've no time to fulfill my order, because a dozen Black Suits surround us. And I've no magic spells left –

The Black Suits point their bayonets at me, yelling at me to freeze with my hands in the air. The V-kids who carry Red stop, put him down, and begin to hiss, ready to attack. In vain I ask them not to put up a fight. The Golem, or Mrs. Snippety Smith, or the pirates, or a bunch of V-kids will come to our rescue.

They don't, and the Black Suits get ever closer, until their odor makes me dizzy. Exhausted and desperate, I crouch over Red's body, hoping to protect him from whatever peril might strike us. Fangs bared, the two V-kids jump on the Black Suits, but to my panic, the enemy slashes them with their bayonets before the vampire children reach their necks.

The Black Suits jerk me off Red and snatch him up with their dark hands. They run away carrying Red's still unconscious body and disappear in an unknown direction.

"Help! The Black Suits have kidnapped Red. Somebody, please. They've got Red!"

The last two Black Suits jump on me, ready to slice me with hatchets. Mortified, I gape at the shiny blades. And that stench nauseates me. I crouch and jump to my left, then to my right, hoping to trick them. But they're right above me. I close my eyes.

There's a blast into the pavement right where I stood a second ago. Maybe it's the hatchets that have just missed me. When I open my eyes, the Black Suits have been pummeled to the ground, the Golem's fist hammering their heads into the sidewalk.

I'm sitting behind the tree, gazing at the puddle of blood where two cherry flowers float now. By the Salem witches' wands! Is Red really gone? He was fighting with me only minutes ago. I start to cry like that time when I realized Mother had been killed. Why do I always lose the people I love?

13. The Mystery of the Black Palace

Another fifty Black Suits surrender, a few dozen run away, and a hundred are dead. But we've also lost two dozen V-kids and even more humans.

Can we ever win this battle?

The Golem ahead catches all the arrows the Black Suits let fly in their ferocious effort to kill me. I'm reassured that we haven't lost control of the fight.

During a noon heat that plasters the armor to our bodies like a second skin, the battle comes to a halt again. The few dozen Black Suits left regroup on the Black Palace's steps, behind a barricade of their fellows' corpses that are making a terrible stench.

I check on my army's casualties. Missing bricks from several stories, the buildings doze in the lingering heat. A few exhausted trees are resting, stripped of their leaves and branches. Streetlamps, their bulbs expired, lie twirled like they're made of rubber.

Their eyes rolling, the V-kids listen to the pirates' stories from the Black, Mediterranean, and Portocalia seas. Others chat with a few wounded humans. By their tears, I realize that some vampire children have found their parents.

Loaded with painkillers, bandages, and sandwiches, the Fortunes and Mrs. Snippety Smith attend to the soldiers' pain, injuries, and hunger. They cover them with blankets, tend their wounds, and feed them magic potions that put many back on their feet, while others linger, dying.

"Let's see if the palace has a secret entrance," I tell the Golem.

He nods and follows me.

We tiptoe around the palace, looking for a back door to slip through. Hoping to discover the enemy's most secret efforts, I already imagine the Golem sending the Black Bug straight to its death – thus ending the battle sooner and avoiding more casualties in my army. But to my surprise and anger, there are no other entries, stairs, or cracks in this sturdy black metallic castle. I'm forced back in a circle to the front stairs, where the dozen Black Suits point their guns at us.

I don't give up. I put my right foot on the first flight of stairs, hoping to sneak into the palace right under the Black Suits' noses. The Golem follows me, glaring ferociously at the enemy.

All goes well until I reach the third step. Suddenly there's a swishing by my left ear. I keep going – until I reach the tenth step. A terrible pang pierces my left shoulder. I'm dizzy, stagger, and before I know it, I've fallen onto the Golem's left foot.

The pain becomes unbearable, and my eyes dim. Waltz and a few V-kids run toward me. I'm getting cold and thirsty, my mouth is dry.

Have I been shot?

Suddenly Mother's face turns up in the sky, then Mr. D's, then everything grows dark.

I open my eyes. It's night again. The falling star shoots all over the sky, like it's gone mad. Waltz, whose head is right above me, licks my face. When my numbness slowly eases, I hear a whistle in my ear. The noise gets louder until it forces me fully awake. I remember now. It's my army's buzz! The V-kids, the fight, my wound. I try to stand up, but waver and fall on my butt.

"What time is it?" I ask.

"Midnight," a V-kid says.

"And the Black Suits?" I ask, amazed that we can sit safely and have a chat on the site of the bloody fight.

"Gone," a familiar voice says.

Zelda! Beautiful in her long cloak made of scales, she tells me that the last dozen Black Suits lying on the palace's steps quit their post upon seeing the latest reinforcement on the vampires' side: Zelda with her deadly fangs.

"Rose and the Midgets sent me as soon as they learned you had been wounded." She says she has put some snake medicine on my injury. "Don't worry, the poison is weak. But we can't take out the bullet. It's stuck."

"What does that mean?"

"It means I'll have to go deep inside your wound to remove it. Besides, if it were not for this pendant--" Zelda hands me pieces from Marga's medallion--"the bullet would've gone straight into your heart."

By the Salem witches' wands! There's nothing left of the medallion except for Marga's sad eyes.

"For now," Waltz says, "the poison has stopped the infection from spreading."

"But you'll feel the pain," Zelda says. "It won't be easy."

I clench my fists and mouth. My teeth are screeching, and my heart is throbbing. There's only one thought in my mind. What if Zelda bites me? She *is* a vampire, after all, and she'll no doubt remove the bullet with her fangs.

"No," I say. I should still be able to do something without having to stand the improvised surgery. But what, since I'm left out of Roma magic?

"No?" Zelda and Waltz ask. "But you'll die."

That cuts short my hesitation. I don't know if I'll be able to stand the pain, but anything is better than dying – even a vampire's bite.

"As she gets closer to my shoulder, Zelda's vampire fangs gleam in the moonlight.

Hissing, she removes my gear. A stream of scarlet-red blood flows from my shoulder. I touch the burned edges of my wound and feel a small hole that goes deep, all the way to the sniper bullet.

Zelda leans over my wound. Her fangs dig into my flesh. The pain is unbearable, and the bullet doesn't seem to budge. Astonished that Zelda is holding her vampire temper so well, I practically forget about the pang. I close my eyes. The twinge becomes really strong, as if an incandescent arrow has punctured my slit.

"Oww!"

Zelda springs backward, her face colored red from my blood. She looks ferocious when she spits out the bullet. "You're a brave little girl," she says.

"Thank you," I say while she smears a healing Roma gel over my wound. She wraps my shoulder in a bandage made of snakeskin.

All the powers that sleep in my body suddenly awaken and put me on my feet. Although my wound hurts badly, I decide to be proud of it. It's a sign that I'm a real warrior. Besides, it's time to meet the Black Bug inside that bleak palace.

Zelda, the Golem, and I climb the stairs, stepping over piles of arrows, bayonets, leaves, and bricks scattered around as if in the aftermath of a terrible tremor. When we reach the hundredth step, a metallic door that bears no signs or carvings opens as if pulled by an invisible hand.

We're in. The door closes behind us with a cavernous boom. Voices buzz, like a chorus imitating a stormy wind. Silver and golden electric currents cross the walls, lighting the darkness. They give me goosebumps and wake up Meow inside my jeans' pocket. But the Golem stares straight ahead, unimpressed by the thunders in the walls.

"I don't like it," Zelda says, wrapping her cloak tighter around her body.

"What do you think is wrong?" I ask.

"I have this feeling," she says, "like this is neither human- nor vampire-made."

Something catches my attention on Zelda's coat. I stare closely at the silver-scale fabric. An eye opens near Zelda's waist.

A snake's eye!

Another frightening eye opens, blinking slowly. Zelda's python is here, with us, disguised as her cloak.

We reach a silver door at the end of the hallway. The Golem pushes it sideways and we proceed along a mounting corridor, empty and dark. Electric thunders pierce the walls like a warning, while the chorus turns into a loud wild cry, probably signaling someone about our trespassing.

Panic slowly seizes my body. The palace is completely empty – there's no single chair, or painting, or table. Or Black Suit.

We keep mounting the slanted tubular corridor until we reach a large round mirror – a dead end. Its silvery surface seems fluid, with impressions of waves that spread toward its edges and return to its center with a plop.

The Golem thrusts his right foot straight at the liquid mirror – and slowly vanishes through it. Both Zelda and I yell at him: "Stop!" His body remains caught in between the hallway and the unknown room or world beyond the fluid mirror.

The deafening chorus stops wailing, and the electric currents withdraw in the metallic black walls.

I press my index finger against the mirror, and it goes all the way through. What if there's someone or something waiting for me on the other side that might bite my finger? I withdraw it, but to my surprise it's not wet.

I do the same with my arm, with the same result. And the Golem is still half with us in the corridor, half vanished on the other side. In the end, since the Golem hasn't melted, or exploded, or turned silver from the liquid mirror, I ask Zelda, "Should we go through?"

Zelda nods, grabs my arm, and before I know it we're on the other side, calling the Golem to follow us.

Inside a pitch-black chamber, a voice roars at us, "Get out of my palace, you unworthy earthlings!"

The Black Bug? My heart pounds in my throat, my stomach churns. I have to summon my herbs-witch courage to take over my shaky body. I hesitate, then say, "Hello?"

No one answers.

Zelda and her python hiss in the dark. The Golem stands perfectly still, his arms and feet spread, ready to fight. I get impatient – I'm exhausted after two days of battle, and my shoulder hurts.

"Black Bug," I dare the unknown enemy, "show your face! All the Black Suits are dead. And now it's your turn."

Booming laughter spreads throughout the dark room. When the sinister cackles cease, Zelda and I edge closer to the Golem, hoping he'll protect us should the Black Bug attack.

A glow shows up in the ceiling. It spreads fuzzy light around the place, revealing a room as large as the Talking-Benches Park. The gleam descends slowly, getting bigger and brighter. There's something dark in its midst. Halfway down, the oval thing wobbles.

A giant cranium!

Zelda and her python fret behind me. With her vampire fangs sticking out, Zelda seems larger and deadlier. The Golem stands ready to fry the suspended apparition.

The fleshless skull has a hole instead of a nose and a mouth with no lips but dozens of yellow teeth. And it glares at me with two sapphires bigger than anything I saw on my voyage to the Sapphire Sea –

Wait a minute. Those must be the Sapphire Sea Dragon's eyes!

Glowing, silvery, and hideous, the cranium stares at me. It opens its mouth and roars, "How dare you stand in front of me?"

Zelda and her python want to jump on the skull.

"Hold them back, Marigold of Salem!" the cranium blasts.

By the Salem witches' wands!

"How do you know my name?" I ask, feeling as small as a sparrow.

"But do you know my name?" the booming voice asks.

"You're the Black Bug," I say. "A tyrant!"

"Ha, ha, ha!" the voice thunders. "You're nothing but a little apprentice who will never become a true witch. Do you think your mother was any better?"

"What do you know about my mother, you ugly head?" My voice gets stronger as my wound spreads pain through my body. "You, who have stolen children and forced Romas to give up their magical ways? You, who have preyed on the forests and the bears and all the other animals? You, who have polluted the waters of Rondelia and destroyed the books? You, who have killed the fairies, the stories and the legends, and stolen the eyes of the Sapphire Sea Dragon?"

The cranium explodes in a blasting laughter while millions of phosphorescent dots light up the room, then turn into golden and silver electric lightnings.

"I'm your worst nightmare," the voice says. "Don't you recognize me?"

I stare, confused.

"I am Queen Nocturna," the cranium says. "Queen Nocturna!"

I freeze. Queen Nocturna of the Land of Endless-Night? Queen Nocturna who killed Mother? My wound hurts badly. But where's the acrid smell? Then it strikes me. That's why she chose to live in a palace made of metal: to hide her stench. If only I knew.

"You and your vampires have killed my children," Queen Nocturna says. "How many Black Suits should I mold from mud to keep this country in order?"

I can't utter a word.

"You and your witches have banned me from Salem." Queen Nocturna's voice sends thunders into the walls. "Salem was mine and mine alone, you boring witches! And now you've come here to bother me again? How dare you?"

"But you killed Mother!" I yell back, unknown courage taking over my body.

Queen Nocturna sends tentacles of mud throughout the room and cracks the walls.

"Your Mother was no good," she says.

I'm so angry I feel like I've turned into a vampire kid. But I have no fangs, I'm no Roma magician. I'm just an apprentice. And how can a mere girl defeat Queen Nocturna?

"It was my greatest pleasure to kill her," Queen Nocturna continues. "And now it's your turn!"

Thunders boom in the darkness. My eyes burn with fever. Tears flow toward my dimpled chin.

"Ha, ha, ha." Queen Nocturna blasts her evil laughter. "But first, I have a surprise for you." She whips a tentacle of mud into the ceiling. "There!"

Hanging from the topmost spot in the room, in a coffin made of glass that rotates slowly, sleeps my dear Red. And his face is as pale as if his body had not a drop of blood left in it.

"Red!" I yell.

"He's mine!" Queen Nocturna says.

"Red!" I try again, desperately hoping he'll wake up.

"He can't hear you," Queen Nocturna says, chuckling. "I took his heart and replaced it with Endless-Night mud. He's forgotten you." She laughs, thundering.

Oh, Red . . .

"But don't worry, I'm taking you too. I'm going to eat you. Right now. I've always enjoyed a taste of sweet teardrops." Her laughter booms.

Queen Nocturna heads for my spot on a spiraling trajectory, pouring clouds of black rain over Zelda and the Golem, which engulfs them in a pond of mud. As she comes closer, she opens her mouth like an abyss. And instead of a palate and throat there's only darkness beyond her teeth.

The colossal cranium is now three feet, two feet, one foot away.

"Motherrr!" I yell as her shadow covers me.

A gate of yellow teeth rises in front of me. By the Salem witches' wands! I'm inside Queen Nocturna's mouth.

The monster tries to chew me with two remaining wisdom teeth, but I'm quicker. Although I can't zigzag in my rabbit style, I can still jump all over her tongue. With my last powers I take refuge on a rubber heap at the back of her mouth and thump on it until I make Queen Nocturna cough, choke, and spit me out.

I lie on the ground, dizzy, my shoulder wound burst open.

Zelda, having swum out of the mud, throws her cloak over my trembling body. She calls the Golem, whose clay body is still caught up in the sticky mud.

"I'm still going to kill you, you little witch!" Queen Nocturna chases me with her words.

I'm at the end of my powers, and my shoulder burns like fire. I keep seeing Mother's eyes in the darkness. I hope she'll understand that I did my best to stand up to her deadly enemy.

Suddenly my palm tickles. My jade-green herbs witch line burns all the way to the pinkie and thumb. It grows into small greenish veins that soon take over my hand and arm. I feel them growing into my wounded shoulder, my torso, my feet. A strange green light glows around my body.

Is this my aura?

Zelda steps back, and her python coils into her silver-scale robe. My greenish light reflects sparkles into the Golem's forehead star.

A force pushes me from below. An invisible hand whisks me up in the air, while I spread my herbs witch aura around the room like a giant firefly.

How can this be? Have I grown a pair of butterfly wings? No. Nothing of the kind buzzes behind me. By the Salem witches' wands! Have I turned into a herbs witch?

With the speed of a bee, I stop right in front of Queen Nocturna's ugly head. "Look at me -- me, Queen Nocturna!" I yell at her like a true witch. "I am the last herbs witch of Salem. You may have killed my mother, but one day, I promise, I'll take all your powers away from you. Then you'll never hurt people and spread evil in Salem and Rondelia."

"Ha, ha, ha! Who do you think you are to dare me, you baby witch, you witchlet?" Queen Nocturna says, spitting mud.

I frown at her, hoping to imitate Mr. D's angry vampire face. But though I may have an aura, I have no fangs, and Queen Nocturna laughs harder.

Slowly, my aura turns to emerald-green, pumping a pleasant heat into my body. It shines brighter until it lights up the darkest corner of this dark room.

I glow like a green sun.

When Queen Nocturna attacks me again with her cavernous mouth all the way open, a heavy thump reverberates throughout my body. I squint through my left eye. Like a rubber shield, my aura has bounced Queen Nocturna to the back of the room, where she twists, weakened, like a ball fizzling out air.

Yippee! You ugly monster – take that for Mother!

The sapphire eyes pop out of Queen Nocturna's head and fall to the floor, where Zelda's python swallows them.

But no miracle works twice – or is it only because I'm really not a herbs witch yet?

My impenetrable green aura diminishes back into my palm. Then, puff! It vanishes. And I'm still ten feet up in the air, with no pair of fairy wings on my back –

I'm falling, and mine is no feather gliding. But before I can sprawl flat to the ground, a shadow covers me again.

The Golem has just grabbed me in his huge fist, closing his fingers on me like a cage.

I lie there like a mouse, peering through the giant's fingers as Queen Nocturna's blind skull moves erratically throughout the room, calling my name, swearing it's going to kill me no matter what.

The Golem thrusts his left fist into the cranium, knocking out its teeth, which scatter like seeds in the wind. Queen Nocturna's waves of mud begin to diminish.

There's a noise from behind. The Golem twists its fist toward the mirror door, where Mr. D's bald head shows up. Upon pushing in his sparkling eyes, pointed ears, and skeletal hands, his cloaks' fluttering sleeves and, last, his worn-out black leather boots, he glares at Queen Nocturna and says, "Don't touch the girl, or I'll kill you!"

Mouth wide open, fangs gleaming, he jumps on the skull – which, under Mr. D's attack, screams and explodes in an orange blaze that enfolds them both.

The flames have spread and a corner of Zelda's cloak catches on fire – which forces the python to slither out of its fabric and through the liquid mirror. Zelda grabs my arm and says, "Hurry, we're done here. Let's get out!"

We leave Queen Nocturna under the combined attacks of Mr. D and the Golem, and dash through corridors all the way back to the palace's door. The fire chases us, the electric walls threaten to fry us, and the chorus screams like mad.

In vain we wait in the outburst of a bruised dawn for Mr. D and the Golem to show up. The Black Palace – surrounded by purple-red flames, clouds of ash, and choking smoke – explodes into a million nails and drops of stinking black mud.

From a puddle, the mud grows into a thick pond, but since the black rain keeps falling, the pond of mud becomes a lake, covering the entire Sadness Square, engulfing all the corpses, bricks, trees, lampposts, bayonets, knives, and slingshots from our battle. It rotates until it turns into a vortex, revolving into a giant whirlpool of mud.

There's a crack, then a boom, then a thunder, and the lake of mud slowly dribbles down, eaten by the earth.

14. Endless-Night

On the way back to the Enchanted Forest, carried in the Romas' wagons – their canopies turned blood red – I've slept on a wool blanket and dreamed that although I could fly like a true Salem herbs witch, Queen Nocturna ultimately ate me.

I wake up and touch my body, happy for proof that I'm out of the nightmare. On a blanket next to me, Waltz is in a state of shock. He keeps mumbling "Red, Red, Red . . ." between healing licks at his scratched paws.

A bruised Mrs. Snippety Smith, her clothes torn and burned, tells us about the humans and V-kids we lost in the fight, whose bodies the spell-casters are burying to rest with the spirits of the Enchanted Forest, but that despite our painful losses we must never forget that we've won and brought freedom to Rondelia.

But at what cost?

We reach the Roma spell-casters' camp. I walk through the pale, late-September grass, listening to the chorus of crickets and the knocking of woodpeckers.

The circus kids dash toward me. "Zaraza is dead, Marigold," they say, their faces desperate.

"What?" I ask.

"She was killed here, in the Enchanted Forest," a circus kid says. Apparently, the Roma spell-casters were chasing some Black Suits who'd taken refuge in the woods. Zaraza was behind them, throwing spells to immobilize their bodies and freeze their minds. But when a lost child from the horse-trainers' camp showed up on a wild horse and a Black Suit aimed at him, leaving her no time to throw any spells, Zaraza jumped in front of the child and took the bullet in her heart. "She died instantly."

"Did Mr. D ever find out?" I ask them, my voice shaky.

"Yes. He'd just recovered and was on his way to Sadness Square, where the fight was at its peak. He stopped here for a while. When we told him Zaraza was dead, he wanted to revive her as a vampire. But at the last moment he found out you were in danger and hurried to the Black Palace."

I close my eyes. There's just too much sadness around me.

The night has sent early shooting stars across the sky to light our way as we're burying Zaraza in the Enchanted Forest.

We warm up at a bonfire, around which Romas from all the clans and from all over Rondelia have gathered. They sing their blue-heart songs, play the dance of death with their knives, trickle a few drops of blood from their fingertips over Zaraza's body, and throw century-old golden coins on her coffin.

A delegation representing the live streetlamps and cherry trees and the citizens of Rondelia sits around the fire. Their faces bruised but proud, the V-kids arrive from the Cathedral. They surround Zelda and Simon-Sea-Phantom and listen enthralled at the pirates' story about how Zelda's python returned the gem eyes to the Sapphire Sea Dragon. Some V-kids say they've found their parents among the human fighters and will go back home. Other vampire children have decided to leave for the Turquoise River Delta, live with Simon-Sea-Phantom's band, become pirates themselves, and visit the Adriatic Sea and Sombreria.

At midnight a commotion wakes me up. The Romas have gathered around a muddy figure with long elongated fingers and yellowish nails. Can it be?

Limping, muddied, and stinking like a Black Suit, Mr. D heads for the campfire. His eyes are bruised like he's been knocked out in a boxing match, and his lip is bloody under one loose fang. His cloak is burned and his fedora hat missing the top.

"I'm fine, I'm fine," he says in a hoarse voice, although he looks pitiful. The V-kids surround him.

"Marigold, how are you doing?" he asks me.

"I thought you were dead," I say.

"Me, dead? Not possible, you know." He laughs and tosses the remnant of his fedora on the grass, where it turns into a castle for a swarming colony of red ants. The entire forest, its creatures and humans, gathers around us.

"Where's the Golem? And what happened to Queen Nocturna?" I ask.

Mr. D explains that Queen Nocturna vanished in a Magic Corridor that opened beneath what was once her Black Palace. She took Mr. D and the Golem with her – "no matter how hard we fought against the tide of mud." The more the Golem burned her with his star beam, the more Mr. D spread poisonous Roma ink on her, the madder Queen Nocturna would get, and she'd smash them with her tentacles of mud. She sucked them into her vortex, but at the last moment the Golem kicked Mr. D out.

"And the Golem?" I ask.

"I lost him," Mr. D says with a dark voice. He suspects that because the Golem is a creature of the past, he was sucked back in time to where he originally came from. "As for Queen Nocturna, she threatened she was going to trickle all the way back to Salem, to the Land of Endless-Night."

My stomach lurches. I feel bad that I never had a chance to thank the Golem. But now it's too late. And if Queen Nocturna took Red with her to Salem, there's no turning back. I have to go to the Land of Endless-Night and rescue him. At least he's still alive, even if he's lost his heart.

But how am I going to tell Mr. D about Red?

I blink and cough gently, my palms sweaty. Just when I'm about to say "Red," a burning thought forces me straight up onto my feet.

"Mr. D," I say, "It's the autumn equinox. Today!"

Mr. D heaves a sigh. "I know."

"But the papyrus said I'd lose my last ancestor when autumn comes." I feel frantic. "Aren't you my great-grandfather? And isn't today September twenty-first?"

"By my father's Dracula blade!" Mr. D says, his face more livid than after a week of blood fasting. "You're right. Marigold. I have to tell you . . . ."

"What?" I say, expecting Mr. D to disintegrate any moment, like Mother.

Mr. D ponders, bites his lips, and frowns. "Listen to me, and don't get scared."

"Why should I get scared?"

Staring into my eyes, Mr. D says, "Because, Marigold, I also am a nocturnal creature"

"What do you mean, nocturnal?"

"I too am made out of night." Mr. D lowers his eyes. "But I'm different."

"From what?"

"From Queen Nocturna."

I'm so astonished I can't say anything for a minute. Finally I put together a sentence.

"I thought only the wicked witches from the Black Hollow Lake and the Black Suits of Rondelia are related to Queen Nocturna."

"Not exactly," Mr. D says with a serious voice. "So are vampires." He explains that vampires are creatures made from the heart of night, a world Queen Nocturna rules over, a world also known as the Land of Endless-Night. "That's who bore us. Queen Nocturna is our mother."

I feel as though the name "Queen Nocturna" has turned into a pick hammer drilling a hole into my head.

"Queen Nocturna, your *mother*?"

"That's right," Mr. D says. "That's why vampires can't stand sunlight."

"But you were human once!" I yell. "You said so."

"True," Mr. D says, "that's why I need your help." He tells me that although he's a vampire, his heart always had a human side, that he's not entirely Endless-Night.

"But great-grandfather, what about me? Am I from Endless-Night too?" My knees tremble.

"No!" Mr. D says. "Remember, Marigold, I told you that only the blood of Dracula princes and of Salem witches flows into your veins – no vampire blood, no Endless-Night."

By the Salem witches' wands!

"That's why I need you, Marigold," Mr. D says, his voice now faint. "You're the only one who can save me now." Mr. D says that once the autumn equinox appoints the Lady of Autumnal Leaves as the ruling season, Queen Nocturna will reclaim his human heart and turn him all Endless-Night. "I won't even recognize you." He looks terrified. "I might even bite you."

That's what probably happened to Red.

But because I'm his last descendant, Mr. D. says, a droplet of my blood – which also belongs to the line of Draculas – can save him, and forever conquer Endless-Night in his heart.

"Just a droplet, Marigold, that's all I need," he says, wrapping his cloak around his body like a cocoon.

"Sure." Then it hits me. Will Mr. D bite me? He's my great-grandfather, but he's also a vampire, and there's Endless-Night in his heart.

The circus kids shows up from behind a pine. Have they been eavesdropping?

"Marigold," the violinist kid says, "or should I call you Princess Maria Dracula?" They bow in front of me, and add a tumble and a salute.

"Marigold is fine," I say, uncomfortable that my Dracula lineage could bite me.

"Silence over silence, over silence, over silence," they say, winking at me.

Who cares about the Mute Woods now? "Yeah, yeah, I know, the silence, the forests – "

"Do you remember the leaf we buried between the junipers?" they ask. "And how we turned it from green to red?"

"Sure, with our blood."

"Like this," they tumble around me, take my right hand, pull out an evergreen pin, and stab my index finger.

"Oww!"

The droplet of blood on my finger reflects in Mr. D eyes. He thrusts his tongue in my direction, although he's three feet away. His tongue extends like a whip and wipes away my blood, like it never existed. Then he licks his lips.

Disgusting! Did he find my blood tasty? And is he going to unleash a full attack on me now?

But Mr. D closes his eyes, and his face whitens. His body shakes like that time when the seizure got him. His fangs clatter and his eyelids flutter.

The circus kids dash to hide in trees, from where they peer at Mr. D through branches and woodpecker holes.

I don't move from my spot. I've risked my life so many times during this trip that a mere vampire fit won't rattle me. Besides, I'm a Salem witch, a Dracula princess, and an Underground combatant. What can scare me now?

A black cloud comes out of Mr. D's nostrils, ears, and mouth. For a while, it floats above his head, as if it wants to go back into Mr. D's body. But in the end it spreads in the chilly night air, hissing, covering the moon.

When he opens his eyes, Mr. D looks relaxed as if he's had a long sleep. And his fangs look stronger than ever.

Yet there's a change. No, it's not his face, or his vampire ears, or his knuckled hands with yellow sharp nails. It's the eyes! Their pupils don't shrink vertically like a cat's but stay round, like a human's.

By the Salem witches' wands! Is he vampire or human now?

Mr. D has difficulties seeing through human eyes and blinks continuously, tears slipping down his face.

But no sooner have his eyes changed than he looks the saddest I've ever seen him – his eyes closed, his lips in a tight line, his brow furrowed.

"What's wrong?" I ask.

"It's Zaraza," he says. "What am I going to do without her?"

What, indeed? It looks like he always loses the woman he loves: first Marga, now Zaraza.

"But you've been given your freedom back," I say.

His face hidden behind his skeletal hands, Mr. D sobs.

But I have a plan. "Mr. D," I say. "Let's go!"

"Where?" Taken by surprise, he peers at me between his fingers.

"To Salem!"

"Marigold, why would I ever want to go there?" He stares at me as if he sees me for the first time.

"Because of Red."

"Red? Why? What's happened to him?" Mr. D falls on the grass, howls like a wolf, and rips his cloak. "Is Red dead?"

I shake my head. "Not exactly." I tell Mr. D about Queen Nocturna and how she turned Red's heart into Endless-Night mud.

"By my father's Dracula blade! In that case, of course," Mr. D says. "Red is my dear boy, I'd do everything to have him back – " He stops, his face panicky. "But Marigold, are you really willing to go into the Land of Endless-Night?"

For Red? Any time. "Yes, and the sooner the better," I say. I call the circus kids from their refuge posts in the trees. "Listen to me, I've learned the secret of the Mute Woods," I say.

"Are you going to tell us?" a kid asks, his eyes bright with wonder.

"Mrs. Snippety Smith told me she landed in those woods -- "

"Mrs. Snippety who? You mean the spy woman?" another circus kid asks.

"She's not a spy. She's a Salem warrior witch," I say.

"Warrior witch?"

"She even knew why there's silence in those woods," I say.

They look at me, amazed.

"It's because of a Magic Corridor that sucks in all the noise of the forest," I say.

"I told you!" the circus kids say one after another, asking who among them thought of the void first.

I interrupt the squabble. "Excuse me," I say, "there's more." The kids shut up and stare at me. "And this corridor goes all the way back to Salem."

They jump around and summersault in their, excitement. I ask them to help me find the Mute Woods again and the entry to the Magic Corridor leading back home.

"Mr. D is coming too," I say.

"What? Did you tell him the secret?"

"No, but if we find the way back to Salem, Mr. D will join me." I tell them that's our plan, and that Mrs. Snippety Smith will surely want to go back home – accompanied by Rose, of course.

Dressed up in a new black cloak and fedora, Mr. D walks in front of the amazed congregation around the fire. He clears his throat, and says, "Ahem. We're leaving for Salem. After five hundred years, I've finally decided to leave these lands and embark on a trip to the New World." He says he'll never regret his glorious exploits as a vampire, although he's often struck with remorse at the thought of the many innocent people he's killed.

But he hopes his work for the Underground and the victory he and all the humans and creatures fighting in the battle against the Black Suits have won can redeem him for good.

"I never thought I'd leave Europe, you know. Five centuries ago people traveled to the ancient worlds of China and India, rarely to the New World."

All the souls around the fire gape at him, still and silent.

Mr. D shows me a reptile leather piece of luggage and a smoky hand – Mr. Shadow's, probably – slipping inside like a black sheet of paper. "I'm also taking the magic lyre, to help us find vampires in the New World, or wherever we might be."

A procession of Romas, V-kids, and pirates follows us as we cross the Enchanted Forest through yellow glades, ponds filled with toads, and fields washed with dew.

When we reach the Mute Woods, the circus kids search for the juniper shrub and the leaf with our oath blood. They find it and hold it up in the air. The green-and-red leaf swings, then directs the kids like a magic guide.

In the solemn silence around us we find a stream where golden fish leap. A giant oak rises in that enchanted place, and a door takes shape in its bark. But there's no plate on it, nor anything else to tell us what kind of door this is or where it can take us. I'll just have to trust the oak! And I wish from the bottom of my heart that the door is the opening to the Magic Corridor back to Salem.

I touch the doorknob, and the bark door suddenly opens and a strong gust sucks Mr. D, Mrs. Snippety Smith, Rose, and me inside the tree.

We're falling into the dark abyss, each of us flying in a bubble of air. From the door above – through which moonlight filters – Zelda and Waltz, the V-kids and the Romas peer down at us, waving their hands, saying goodbye.

Just when we pop out into the Milky Way galaxy, I feel my eyelids getting heavier and heavier. My companions have already fallen into a magical sleep. Mr. D looks like a spider with his arms, legs, and cloak spread in the air; Mrs. Snippety Smith's hair has turned silvery like the stars around us; little Rose's head is cradled in her drawing notebook.

A star from the Heroes' Black Hole twinkles at me. I wave back at the Golem star, saying goodbye, happy you got back home.

Mother, where are you?

I don't have to wait long. The falling star of the Aquarius constellation shows up and catches us on her foam tail, carrying us further into the galaxy. As I'm falling asleep, I have no doubt that Mother has found me and we're heading back home.

I close my eyes, and all of a sudden Red and Waltz, Simon-Sea-Phantom and Zelda, the pirates and the Sapphire Sea Dragon, the dolphins and Romas surround me. They're all there, in my dream. And in my heart, where they'll always be.

~ *To be continued* ~

175

Maria Dracula and the Land of Endless-Night

Three years have passed since Marigold has returned to Salem.

Now she prepares to take the Witchcraft Test and assume her powers as the last Grand Herbs Witch of Salem.

But she never forgot Red, how could she? Still, she never found him, for nobody knew where heartless Queen Nocturna had taken refuge upon her trickled return from Rondelia.

Purple grapes and burgundy leaves cover Salem. As nights grow longer, Mayor Icelandia de Winter summons the Lady of Autumnal Leaves to take over the last months of the year.

But on Halloween night, the Black Hollow Lake resonates with a strong commotion no witch can explain. At midnight the wicked witches attack Salem, forcing it back to the Land of Endless-Night.

Everything seems lost.

Will the witches of Salem, Marigold, and Mr. D succeed in fighting these powerful enemies? Will Marigold ever find Red?